In Love With a Miami Billionaire

Billionaire

TINA J

You Can Follow Me At:

Facebook Author T M Jenkins
Instagram Author Tina J
Instagram Tina J Presents
Twitter Author Tina J

www.tjpresents.com

Foreword

There are two wolves in each one of us. A Black Wolf and a White Wolf. The White wolf thrives on Love and Faith. The Black one is full of Fear and Hate. You have to know which one to feed, and when.

Godfrey
 Knightfall

CHAPTER 1

Zakiya

"My back is killing me girl." I said to Andrina, who started working in this dead-end job with me seven months ago.

We worked in housekeeping at the Four Seasons which is one of the hottest hotels in Miami. I've seen a ton of celebrities in this place, along with the top drug dealers, so called kingpins and plugs too. Most of them with their women, groupies and in some cases; side chicks and mistresses. You name it, I've seen it. Five years of working here; I guess I would.

I also worked part time in the hotel restaurant on occasion. I tried to get as many hours possible but sometimes, it's not worth it because minimum wage is low and unless you get a rich person in here, you may bring home $30 a night. People are cheap as hell and it shows even after we clean the hell outta their rooms or bring their food out hot. I know times is hard but damn.

Anyway, Andrina and I, hit it off and became tight. Her aura and energy are always positive and with all the negative people in my life, it was needed. From the shootings every night, to the robbery's, rapes and murders, I wanted some hope and she's so bubbly it definitely uplifts me everyday.

Liberty city manor in Miami is where I grew up at and still reside due to being broke. We moved here fifteen years ago when I was eleven years old, with my mom and stepfather, thinking it would be good but nope, it was the exact opposite.

Yea, I work and because I do, housing goes off my income which does seem like a lot when you check out the gross but my ass ain't bringing that home. By the time the government rape me in taxes, I have just enough to pay rent, buy some food and get my hair and nails done.

I may shop at Walmart, Target and even Family Dollar at time for clothes, but my head, feet and nails are always done. I'm not looking for anyone; however; I don't have to look a hot mess either. It helps that I can do my own weave and wigs too. No, I'm not a hair stylist: nor do I wanna be one.

Growing up my dusty ass, crackhead, smoking the pipe, shooting heroin ass momma always tricked our food stamps and money away. Therefore; I'd steal from the beauty supply stores or rob one of my teachers when they left the class to use the bathroom, after the bell rung just to buy some. Living in the projects are rough and trying to do better is worse.

I mean shit, I have my own apartment and the small things I did purchase with the tips, were from thrift stores. The only two things I did get from rent a center, was a living room and bedroom set. I refuse to have my place looking crazy.

The good thing is, I lived in the back apartments where a lot of the older folks lived. No one really bothered me, and I begged the manager to put bars on my window since it's on the first floor. It took some persuading, but a bitch had to do what was needed to stay safe.

Unfortunately, I gave in and used what I had, to get what I wanted from the manger a few times. Call me a hoe all you want; I call it survival and in order to live here, it's the only mode you had to stay in.

"Mine too but you know the job has to be done if we wanna get outta here." I blew my breath and pushed the cart to the next room.

I was cool with the manager Jerry, so when Andrina and I became close, I asked if we could work as a buddy system. It kept us safe and we could gossip about the nasty people who stayed here.

This hotel is top notch, and you can't imagine the disgusting things they do and leave for us to clean. One time, Andrina and I had to clean the twentieth floor and we were excited. Shit, it's where the penthouse is, along with a rooftop pool, bar and on the other side, is a club. Yup, a damn club.

They say, the owner only partied with celebrities and the Elite. He didn't want them to feel like they were under a microscope if they wanted to party, so he built a club. You couldn't even get in unless you stayed on the twelfth floor and up. Those were the most expensive to stay on.

In any case, Andrina and I took our carts and went to clean it. Little did we know, they had a party the night before and it was trashed. I'm talking condom wrappers left on the floor with sperm still in it, weaves, pills, bottles, and one couple was still up and fucking in the pool.

I'm telling you it was disgusting and any time we had to do the clean-up now, we had to take six other people because it took the two of us five hours to clean.

"Bitchhhhhhh, look at this." Andrina shouted from across the hall. We kept the doors opened with stoppers just in case. I ran over and my eyes almost fell out my socket.

"You think we should touch it?" She asked and walked over to the three suitcases open and full of money on the bed.

"Are you fucking crazy? You know the type of people who stay here." I glanced around the room and there was a Rolex, a couple diamond rings, three cell phones and two laptops.

"Zakiya, look at all this money." She lifted one up and let it make that noise when you flip through it.

"Put that shit down and let's go." I snatched her by the wrist.

"AHHHHH!" We heard and turned to see a body falling passed the window. We looked at each other and ran over.

"You think he made it?" She asked.

"We on the fourteenth floor and he was up higher than us. Hell no he ain't make it." We pushed our foreheads further in the window tryna see down and couldn't.

"AHHHH!" Another body passed in front of us and I almost had a damn heart attack.

"Let's get the fuck outta here." We started running to the door and stopped short when two men, with big black, long guns stood there.

"I think I just sharted." Drina looked at me.

"What the hell is sharted?" She whispered as the two men never moved. I don't even think they blinked.

"When you fart and shit a little." I spoke out the side of my mouth quietly.

"You nasty."

"Bitch, I'm about to pee next." My insides were a mess right now.

"Zakiya, you better fucking not."

"Drina, you know my nerves are bad. I live in the hood and hear gunshots all night. To have one pointed at me got my stomach in knots. Oh no!" I shrieked.

"What?" I started walking towards the bathroom.

"You leaving me with these maniacs?"

"I can't hold it Drina. Come with me." I said inching towards the bathroom.

"Don't move bitch." One of the guys said.

"I'm sorry. If I stand here, the room is going to smell like diarrhea." One of the guys turned his face up while the other one told him to watch me. I jogged in one place when I reached the bathroom and unbuckled my jeans.

"Please don't let me shit on myself. Please God." I turned around and poop fell out my ass before I even sat.

"Ooooh Lord, my stomach hurts." I was bent over holding it.

"GOT DAMN YOU STINK BITCH! WHAT THE FUCK YOU EAT?" The guy said and slammed the door.

"Is that her smelling like that?" I could hear them out there.

"DRINA! YOU OK?"

BOOM! I heard and the door busted open.

"Motherfucker you didn't have to throw me into the door."

"You lucky that's all I did. Sit in here with your stinking ass friend and don't come out."

"Fuck you." I yelled. Drina started crying like the baby she is.

"It's going to be ok. SPLASH!" She looked up when my poop hit the water.

"Oh my God. I'm gonna be sick." She tried to open the door, but someone was holding onto it.

"I can't breathe in here. Please let me out." She was banging on it.

"Bitch, I used the air freshener and I'm flushing every time I go."

"That shit ain't working. Ughhh." She started gagging and a few seconds later, vomited in the sink.

SPLASH! When she heard the water in the toilet again, she started kicking the door.

"Stop Drina. They're gonna kill us."

"Have you smelled yourself? I feel like I'm already dead. Now my clothes gonna smell like shit. I gotta get outta here." She continued kicking and banging on the door a few times.

BOOM! The noise was loud so we both covered our mouths. She had her shirt over her nose and tried her best not to smell me.

"I'm sorry Drina. I had to go. Turn around so I can wipe." She did and afterwards I washed my hands really good, then dried them off.

"It's quiet. You think they left." Drina asked and I slowly opened the door. We stepped out and no one was in the room and everything we saw, was gone. I didn't even care where it went. All I wanted to do is finish this shift and go home.

"Next time don't walk in and close the door." I told Drina as we left the room and she helped me do the one across the hall.

"You think they'll come back?" I walked to the cart to grab garbage bags.

"I doubt it. They...." I looked down the hall and a tall man stood there dressed in black staring. Instead of showing fear, I waved.

"Can I help you?" The person headed towards me quickly.

"Sir. Can I help you?"

"Who you talking too?" Drina asked and the person stopped. When she came to the door, the person turned around.

"Let's hurry up. It's too much craziness going on tonight." I pulled the cart in, and the two of us did each room together with the carts inside and doors locked. Whatever went down in this hotel tonight, didn't have shit to do with me and I ain't seen nothing.

CHAPTER 2

Andrina

"Right there Drina. Got damn, I'm about to cum. Fuck woman." I was popping my pussy real good for this guy I've been messing with for the past four and a half months. Tonight, is the first time we had sex and I was making sure to leave a good impression. After giving one another fore play, we've been at it like rabbits.

"Cum for me daddy."

"You do the same. That clit hard as fuck right now." I rode him faster; he circled my treasure and sure enough he exploded in the third condom and I released all over him.

"I needed that." I fell on his chest. My hair was all over the place and we were sweating like crazy.

"You needed that huh?" I asked still tryna catch my breath.

"You know I'm on the road a lot so…"

"Please. I haven't given you any and I know one week is like a year to men. Hell, some can't even wait a day." He laughed and moved my hair out the way.

"How long you staying?" I asked and got up to shower.

"A few days. You working?" He walked in behind me.

"Yea. No one is gonna pay these bills for me." I reached for the shower handle and my body was swung around.

"I told you, anything you need, I got you." I smiled at this handsome man in front of me. He was way past gorgeous, more than beautiful and just such an amazing person.

"We're not a couple and what do I look like having a man pay my bills when I only see him a few times a month?" I stepped in the shower and adjusted the water.

"What are you afraid of Andrina? Are you scared to fall for me or something?" I felt his body behind and everything seemed perfect. His touch, his smell and his love making is so addictive. How could I not find myself falling for him? The only problem is, he's not around enough and I know in my heart, I'm not the only woman in his life.

Granted, no one calls him when we're together but that means nothing. She could live elsewhere or told not to call when he's away. He does answer when I call, even if it's in the middle of the night; yet, I'm not secure with him only being mine. He has a bad boy persona on the outside and like I stated before, he's handsome.

His light brown eyes, perfect build, bowlegs and I love a man with tattoos, and his body is filled with them. Neck to ankles are all different types and I became so fascinated by them, I had him take me to a parlor to get one. I wanted a long stem of roses going down my leg but when the artist turned that damn needle on, I chickened out and settled for a tiny heart. He laughed the whole time.

Anyway, I found myself intimidated when we were out at times due to some of the women. We'd be out having lunch or even dinner and women would break their necks to stare. A couple chicks were bold enough to ask if he were famous or had a brother who resembles him. Anything to start a conversation.

"I don't want to get hurt." He made me face him.

"Hurt? Why would I hurt you?"

"I'm not saying it would be intentional." He lifted my face so our eyes could meet.

"Then what are you saying?"

"I'm 25, live in a small one bedroom outside the hood but still close to it. I drive a 2013 Hyundai Sonata and I work a dead-end job because I got fired from the job my father picked out for me." I chuckled at the last part.

My dad worked at an oil corporation on the finance floor. He got me hired as a secretary for one of the lawyers who represented the company. One day, I was at work taking notes for him when another associate stepped in and whispered something in his ear. He excused himself and told me we could finish later.

I picked my things up and whoever the man was, stood behind me and started rubbing himself on my ass. I pushed him off and he threw me up against the wall making me hit my head. I slid down the wall and woke up to cops in my face asking why I attacked the guy for not wanting me? I had no idea what happened and sadly, in order for the company not to press charges, I had to leave right away.

My father was furious and blamed me. He had the audacity to say, *I almost had him fired since he's the one who vouched for me to work there.* I couldn't believe it; especially when I've only had sex with one man and I'm very shy and timid.

Don't get me wrong, I speak to men, but I won't have sex with a man if he can't wait; hence the reason I've only been with one other guy. These days all men want is sex and need it after only a week of knowing you.

"Fuck that job and your pops. He dead ass wrong. Say the word and he's gone." His face tightened. He hated to see me upset or to hear me even discussing bad things that happened to me.

"Calm down killa."

"You have no idea who you're dealing with Andrina." He took the rag out my hand and washed me gently.

"You're right and it's why I can't allow you to do anything for me." He sucked his teeth.

"We have so much more learning to do about one another." I stared down at him.

"It's going on four months and I'm falling for you and I'm scared." He gave me a hard stare before speaking.

"You should be because once I give you my heart and you break it; you'll won't live to tell a soul." I stopped him from washing me up and looked in his eyes.

"You plan on giving me your heart?" Forget how he'll kill me if I hurt him. I'm shocked he's ok with giving me his heart.

"One day." We finished, threw some pajamas on, ordered food and watched a movie. When I woke up, he was gone. I wasn't mad because this is the type of relationship we have, which is why I know he's not ready to settle down. His ass can't even keep still.

* * *

"Guess he showed up." Zakiya said walking in Walmart with me. We drove our own vehicles here because she's going to work at the hotel restaurant afterwards and I'm going back home.

"Why you say that?"

"This bitch." She pointed to a hickey on my neck. I knew it was there because I'm so light, you can see everything on me.

"Whatever."

"Whatever my ass. I hope y'all used condoms because auntie live in the hood and I can't be babysitting there." She looked at me and we both busted out laughing.

"I hope they have stuff out in here." I complained pulling a shopping cart apart from the others.

"They ain't never got shit on the shelves. Makes me wonder what the staff doing at night." I shook my head and went down a few aisles to grab snacks and canned goods. I grabbed my meats from Whole Foods and sometimes Publix.

"GOT DAMN BITCH! HE FINE AS FUCK!" She damn near shouted making people turn around; including the guy she spoke of. He stood there with a woman who had a perfect shape, expensive looking clothes on and one of those long weaves the women wore.

"I think he heard you." I spoke low.

"He may have. Let's go this way." She turned my cart from the end so we could go down a different aisle.

"Excuse us." Some huge guy blocked off the paper towel aisle.

"You're excused." He responded.

"Can you move?" Zakiya said and tried to push past him.

"Boss is down there, and he wants to shop in private." We looked at each other.

"If he wanted to shop in private, he should've come overnight since the store open twenty-four hours."

"Look. We don't want no problems. Give him a few minutes and you can get what you need."

"A few minutes. You have got to be kidding me." Zakiya had her hands on her hips.

"Is he a celebrity or something? Even if he is, tell him to hurry the hell up. Normal people like us have to work." He kept his eyes straight ahead and stood in a stance with his feet spread apart.

"Fuck this."

"No Zakiya." I watched her pretend to kick him in the balls, which made him close his legs and grab himself, giving her room to run down the aisle to get the tissue and Clorox wipes. She grabbed them and went down the other way.

"Excuse me." I heard in the next section and saw my friend and the guy standing face to face.

"The next time he tells you to wait; do what the fuck he says." His voice spoke volumes even though it wasn't loud.

"I don't have to do shit. What you should've done is brought yo ass here when it's late. That way, no one would be around you. Let's go." Next thing I knew, Zakiya had a gun under her chin and her feet were off the ground.

"What were you saying?" I ran from around the cart.

"Let her go." I went to touch him, and the chick put a gun to my head.

"Ok. We get it. She's sorry. Please let her go."

"Not much to say now huh?" Zakiya shook her head no.

"That's what the fuck I thought."

BOOM! Her body hit the ground and the chick backed up.

"Motherf...." I covered her mouth.

"I don't usually put my hands on women but a bitch will always get dealt with." I still had my hand on Zakiya's mouth as she tried to move it.

"The next time you're in my presence, go the other way." He put his weapon away and I removed my hand from her mouth.

"You can't tell me what to do." She sassed getting up.

"I should press charges. I think my tailbone is broke." She was bent over holding it.

"Keep talking and your jaw will be broke." He nodded and that same big dude made his presence known.

"Respect me or I guarantee, you won't make it to another day." The way he said it sent chills down my spine. Zakiya must've felt the same because she went mute all of a sudden.

"Get those bitches outta my face." Before I could ask who he calling a bitch, both of us were pushed in the other direction so hard, we had to hold on to the shelf to keep from hitting the floor. Neither of us said a word, speed walked to the register and checked out.

"We almost died twice in a week. Lord, keep us safe." She said and hopped in her car. I did the same and drove home wondering where the hell did this guy, and the people from the hotel come from. They were crazy.

"Hey." I answered when my boo called.

"I'll be there in a few. You hungry?" I told him yea and what I wanted from the Chinese place. I hope he stays all night or at least until I dose off. It's been a crazy few days and I needed him next to me.

CHAPTER 3

Consequence 'Con' Waters

"**W**hat the fuck is wrong with y'all pulling guns out in the middle of Walmart?" My mother barked when I stepped through the door of her house.

"Ma, the bitch was disrespectful." I moved past her.

"Disrespectful Consequence? What's disrespectful because let you tell it, a woman can say *excuse me* and if it's not the way you think she should say it, it's disrespectful." I turned and she had her arms folded. All I could do is burst into a fit of laughter. My mother knew me too well.

"I fucking knew it. You probably ain't had no pussy and took it out on the woman at the store." She shook her head.

"What I tell you about talking like that ma?" She's from the hood, well we all are in some way, but she only turned the ratchetness off in public. At home, it's fair game and you never knew what would slip out between her two lips.

"I don't care boy. Got your sister calling me to say, Rock yelling at her because she had to explain why he was told, she's pulling out a strap while carrying his child. You know that nigga don't play about her." She walked ahead of me talking shit.

"He'll be a'ight. Where pops?"

"In his office smoking that nasty ass cigar." I changed direction and went towards the office and stopped when I heard my brother Rage on the phone.

"Babe, I'm not tryna sit in the dirty ass movie theatre to watch some corny romance."

"Babe?" I questioned from behind making him jump. I knew he was dealing with a chick but didn't know they were official.

"Let me call you back." He disconnected the call.

"Why you hang up with babe?" I joked.

"Fuck you punk. Out here doing stick ups in Walmart."

"What the fuck eva. The bitch should've waited like Ron told her." I shrugged. Ron is my security and has been my boy since the middle school.

He went to jail for 7 years for manslaughter at the age of fourteen. The person he killed, was a man he caught beating on his mother. Even though his lawyer determined beyond a reasonable doubt it was self-defense, the judge still made him do time because he had two strikes already.

He stayed in trouble for petty robberies and was convicted twice for having paraphernalia on him, so the judge made an example. It didn't matter because once he stepped foot outside the prison, I had a job for him.

He didn't wanna touch drugs, so I offered for his ass to be my bodyguard. He was 6'5 and weighs at least 320. It worked out perfect and I haven't had any issues with him by my side.

"Nigga, we supposed to keep a low profile, not show our ass over a woman who didn't say *excuse me* the way you wanted her too." He used air quotes too.

"I wish Cee stop telling y'all that lie."

"Lie? What happened then?"

"Ron told her to wait a minute while we were in an aisle and the bitch didn't listen. She started talking shit about how ain't nobody gonna tell her shit, and being the good man, I am, it was only right to show her I meant business." He was doubled over in laugher as I kept a straight face telling my story.

"She's lucky I didn't catch her outside and really make an example."

"Why didn't you?"

"The only reason I didn't is because Ron pushed them so hard, they hit the shelf. When they went to the register I had to laugh because the two of them were quiet as hell and even speed walked out the store." He was hysterical by now and I had to chuckle myself. It sounded funny now that it's over.

"I tell you what, the bitch better go in the opposite direction if she ever graces my presence again." I said in a firm tone making him stop laughing.

"Bro. Every woman isn't Lauren. You gotta let it go. Besides the bitch won't ever return." My face tightened up at the sound of her name and just like that, the joking man I was a moment ago, turned back into the violent crazed maniac I am.

"Baby listen. It's not what it looks like." Lauren said in front of me as she stood there naked.

Her beautiful brown eyes I loved and facial expression told an entirely different story. Her perfect shaped body I had done for her was covered with something sticky and the tassels hanging from her breast made the scene worse. Not to mention a pair of men sneakers sitting next to the front door.

We've been together for six years and this particular house was built for her. It had wall to wall carpet, and she hated for anyone to walk in with shoes on; therefore, you always had to take them off.

"Move." I pushed her to the side and stomped my way through the house looking for the mystery guy who was experiencing a woman who had my last name; my son and now my unborn child in her stomach and the key to my heart.

"Consequence please listen to me." I stopped at the bedroom door with my hand on the doorknob.

"WHAT THE FUCK DO YOU WANT?" I shouted with my back still turned. I'm not sure what I'd do if I faced her.

"Don't kill him. It's not his fault." Instead of responding, I turned the handle and proceeded to walk in, only to be met with a gun to my face.

I stared at the guy, then the unmade bed, back to her and then him. Rage immediately took over and all my common sense went out the window.

I knocked the gun out his hand and began beating him until his face was unrecognizable. I drug his body down the stairs, not *caring if blood was dripping on the carpet or not, opened the back door and dropped him.*

"OH MY GOD!" Lauren ran out to see what I did, and I could care less. I walked to the shed I kept my tools in and grabbed the gasoline and blowtorch.

"Consequence what are you about to do?" She asked trying to get in front of me.

"I'm about to light this nigga on fire first, then this house and if you still here when it's all said and done, I'ma light yo ass up too." She watched me pour the gasoline on the dude, outside the house and over her car.

"Consequence."

"BITCH YOU STILL HERE?" I question and turned the knob on the blowtorch and lit everything up. She covered her mouth and backed away.

"I told you to leave." I snatched her up, tossed her in the back of my truck, put child locks on and drove away.

"Consequence please don't hurt me." I stopped short and half of her body was in the front of my truck.

"You got some got damn nerve." I pulled off again and sent a text out to someone I knew who owed me a favor.

"Just tell me why? That's all I need to know. Why?" I'm the type of nigga who needed an explanation as to why people did dumb shit.

"He was my ex when I lived in Florida. He came to visit, and I agreed to have lunch with him. Long story short, he followed me home and you walked in after we finished." I let my eyes meet hers in the rear-view mirror and shook my head.

"That's the dumbest shit I've heard today. Try again." She didn't say anything. I snatched her up by the hair and had her head in between the console.

"Why?"

"He was going to kill me if I didn't tell him about your businesses." I'm not into the streets and I damn sure don't sell drugs so why would she say, that's why he's here?

"So you fuck him instead of telling me? Again, sounds dumb. Try again." I gripped her hair tighter.

"Ok. Ok. The bitch Lisa called my phone and said y'all were still sleeping together. She sent photos of you and her out and I wanted to get you back. How could you cheat Consequence?" I let go and pulled in at the clinic and parked in the back.

Lisa is a woman I slept with off and on when Lauren and I would go through something. Once we got married, regardless of what we went through I never cheated so she's lying. I did let her suck me off a few times because she was better at it than my wife. However; I never stuck my dick in her as a married man.

"Let's go." I pulled up in the parking lot.

"Why are we here?" I yanked her out, drug her to the back door and knocked. This guy I went to school with, his wife is a gynecologist and performed abortions. Of course, this isn't what I wanted to do, but I don't give a fuck at this point.

"We ready." She said and shook her head after seeing Lauren. Everyone knew the type of man I was, so no one ever asked questions.

A half hour later, Lauren walked out of the clinic in a hospital gown, netted draws, and minus a baby.

"Are you taking me home?" She asked in a weak voice.

"If I take you anywhere, it will be to a lake to drown you." Horror came over her face.

"If I ever see your face again, I'll cut your throat." I got in and pressed the gas.

BOOM! I hit the bitch with the side of my truck, and I haven't seen her since.

"What the hell happened?" My mom's voice broke me outta my thoughts. I looked down and the window in my father's office was no longer there.

"You know how he gets when the bitch Lauren name comes out. He gets all crazy and throws shit. Look at my damn recliner on the lawn." My father said shaking his head.

"Stop bringing the ho up then. Got my son all upset. What if my grand baby woke up?" She slammed the door and my brother and father looked at me.

"Well alright then. Can we discuss business now?" I apologized to my pops, grabbed a drink from the bar and leaned against the wall.

I hated that bitch for cheating and even more for not taking care of our son. I did tell her not to ever show her face again, but she hasn't called, sent gifts or anything.

I should've killed her when I had the chance. At least, I could've told my son she died in a car accident. *Dumb bitch.*

CHAPTER 4

Zakiya

"Thank you for coming to the Four Seasons, how can I help you?" I heard the chick at the front desk say as I walked behind her to punch in.

"I'm good. Where's Mr. Connors?" The voice said and I froze. It's no way in hell, the man from Walmart is here.

It's been a little over a month since my near-death experience and I haven't slept good yet. Every time I close my eyes, I see the gun under my chin and the hateful look on the man's face. The shit would invade my mind right away.

"He's in the main conference room sir. Would you like me to inform him that you're here?"

"Did I ask you to do that?" He snapped.

"No sir."

"Ok then. Don't ask me no dumb ass questions. And fix your name tag; it's crooked. How the fuck somebody supposed to read your name and it's crooked?"

"I apologize. I must've..."

"Did I ask for an excuse?" He barked and I stepped out putting my hair up.

"Why the fuck are you coming from the back? You get paid to make yourself up?" He barked at me.

"Who the hell he talking to?" I looked at the chick who was about to cry.

"This is..." She tried to tell me something and he cut her off.

"Did I tell you to mention my name?" He barked again.

"First of all... whoever you are, don't bring your ass into this establishment disrespecting and intimidating the staff. Second... what I do at my job, is none of your got damn business." His face tightened.

"We're waiting on you Mr. Waters." Some woman said coming out the downstairs conference room.

"And third... don't you have somewhere to be?" His eyes now had slits in them.

"Bye." I waved him off and escorted the chick in the back to comfort her.

"He's so means every time he comes here." I shook my head. He's an ass everywhere.

"Miss Zakiya. Can you come out here for a minute?" I heard my boss Jerry say. She's cool as hell and I loved working for her. I stepped out and noticed a nervous look on her face.

"Yea." I fixed my uniform.

"I need you to punch out. You're suspended for two weeks."

"Come again." I had to be hearing things.

"You were observed being rude and hostile towards a customer. I'm sorry but it's outta my hands."

"Are you joking?" She shook her head no.

I stormed in the back, punched out and went straight to the conference room. I barged in and the person I wanted to speak to wasn't anywhere in sight. Everyone looked at me crazy. I apologized and backed out the door.

"See yo ass in two weeks and your attitude better be different." He said leaning on the wall.

I was mad at myself for allowing him to make me get suspended for two weeks and mad at myself, for lusting after this beautiful, arrogant, ignorant and demon like person.

He stood at about 6'3 if not taller with a decent build but I can't really tell. His clothes were definitely expensive and so were his shoes. Those hazel eyes pierced straight through me today, the same as they did at Walmart.

What the hell is he doing that's captivating me; drawing me to him? Is it his rude demeanor? His looks, or the fact his aura screams RESPECT ME OR ELSE? Whatever the case, I'm turned off and intrigued at the same time.

"I had so much to say but I see now, it's no need. Move." I pushed past him and once again, my body was thrown against something. At Walmart it was the shelf, here it's the spot in between the two elevators.

"Ouch. You made my back hit the elevator button." He stared at me and for a quick second, I thought he smiled. Then he opened his mouth and I almost shit on myself.

"Your mouth is going to be the death of you." He tossed me out the way and I fell into one of the lobby chairs.

I watched him walk down the hall and disappear into the conference room. That man is crazy but I'm game. At least, he didn't put a gun under my chin. I got myself together and went home.

* * *

"I think he wants you." Drina said as we sat in a sports bar drinking.

"Girl bye. The man clearly has female issues if he has no problem putting his hands on them." I picked up a fry.

"Technically, he didn't hit you."

"Bitch, he pushed me up against a shelf, dropped me on the floor, had his guard push me again, threw me against an elevator wall and then a chair."

"Again. Technically he didn't hit you." I gave her a death look.

"He did throw you around like a rag doll tho." She shrugged and both of us directed our attention to some women yelling.

"Probably arguing over some nigga." Drina said and we finished eating and talking.

As the two of us were about to walk out the door, five women walked up to one chick who was sitting alone. The woman had her back turned so we couldn't see who she was.

One of the chicks started popping mad shit in her face. The whole place started paying attention.

"Oh shit Zakiya. That's the bitch who put the gun to my head." Now we were really being nosy.

"You think he gonna be faithful? Nah boo. He knows we won't ever be over. This pussy got him strung out." The girl stared patting the top of her jeans.

"Ratchet ass bitches I swear." The woman who was alone said loud enough for the chick to hear.

"Ratchet? Bitch we about to whoop yo ass in here." The woman wasn't saying much but you could tell she was mad.

All of a sudden, the manager and a few of the bus boys emerged from the back. He asked all of them to leave and being nosy, we followed.

"They about to jump her." Drina said.

"Yup and we about to watch." She laughed. The ratchet chick swung, and the girl beat the brakes off her.

"Fuck you and that baby." The ratchet chick screamed out after getting beat up.

"BABY!" We said at the same time. The ratchet chick friend went to their car and you could see her put a knife or something in her hand.

"We can't let them jump her." Drina said and threw her hair in a quick braid.

"Why the fuck not?"

"She's pregnant Zakiya. I bet whoever the chick mess with, is pregnant by the guy the ratchet girl used to mess with. You know the ex can never let go."

"True but fuck that. The bitch pulled a gun on you."

"We can't worry about that right now. Look, she's on the phone with her back turned. The bitch running up to her."

"You owe me." We dropped our shit and intervened before they could swing on the pregnant girl. Drina and I ain't no slouch and were going toe to toe with these bitches.

"Bitch, did you bite me?" I asked one who I slammed on the ground and stomped on her face. She grabbed my leg and sunk her teeth into it. I started stomping her again.

"Drina we gotta go." I shouted after hearing cop cars. She was slamming some girl head into the ground.

We ran to the car and I saw two black trucks with tinted windows pull up and on our way out the parking out, four cop cars pulled in.

"I hope they don't snitch."

"Like I said. You owe me." I told Drina and kept checking my rear-view mirrors.

"Owe you for what?"

"I almost got my ass beat by some man twice, and then you had me fighting in a parking lot to help some bitch we don't even know."

"You know damn well you would've felt some kind of way had we not stepped in." I waved her off. She's right. I never wanted to see anyone get jumped and I wasn't about to let a pregnant woman go through it either.

It just goes to show you bitches always talking shit but ain't really bout it when the time comes. It's why they bring friends.

They know it's a possibility they'll lose and don't wanna be clowned. Niggas do it too.

"Have fun at work tomorrow."

"Ugh ahh bitch. I told Jerry my family had an emergency in Asia, and I had to take two weeks off." I busted out laughing.

"I wish I would work there without you."

"Awww. I love you sis." I had mad love for Drina, and she showed me she felt the same.

I dropped her off and drove to Walgreens to grab some Zzquil to help me sleep. I stepped out the store and some big black guy blocked the entrance.

"Excuse me." I tried to go around and he kept me there.

"What the fuck wrong with you? You can't hear? Move nigga." He stepped aside and some guy stood there looking down on his phone. When his eyes met mine, he seemed familiar, but I couldn't place him.

"What's your name?"

"None of your got damn business. Move." He gripped my arm tight.

"What is with the men out here? Each one of you have hand problems. Get the fuck off." He chuckled and tossed me to the side.

"Bitch, I just wanted to say thank you for making sure those bitches didn't stab my peoples. Where's the other chick?"

"If you followed me here, you should've saw where I dropped her off at." The knife was at my throat so fast, if I moved, I'd cut my own shit.

"All you had to say is you're welcome and I'll let my friend know."

"You're welcome and I'll tell her." He took the knife away.

"Your mouth is mad reckless. I suggest you ask about me." I just nodded and waited for him to leave. How am I supposed to ask about him and he didn't leave his name?

I rushed to my car, made sure they weren't following me and drove home. My hands were shaking, tears were falling down my face and all I could think of was holding in this poop that was struggling to stay in. If I never have to see him, his peoples or that other guy ever again in my life, I'll be just fine.

CHAPTER 5

Courageous 'Rage' Waters

"Who taught yo sexy ass how to strip?" I let my hands run up shorty legs. Her body was swaying with the beat and her ass bounced along with it as well. This woman was gorgeous to me; inside and out.

She's smart, sophisticated and has her own place, which a lotta women have these days. The difference is, no matter how much I offered to drop money on her, she refused each time. To me, it shows independence and strength because she could have whatever she wanted from me just by saying yes and she chose not to. I think it's why my feelings are beginning to run deep for her.

"No one taught me and if you said I wasn't doing it right, then I'd know not to ever do it again." The song went off.

Another one came on and she sat on my lap facing me. She smiled and her eyes went into a slant due to her being mixed.

Her mom is Asian and her pops is black and one of those Uncle Tom motherfuckers who rather put his family down then to look out for them.

"You should know you did it right. Look." I pointed to my erection in my basketball shorts.

"I guess, I know something you like." Her body began to move in circles. My shorts were still on and I felt wetness coming through.

"You wet for me?"

"Yes baby. Always." Her hand went inside my shorts, pulled my man out and let the tip touch her clit. I reached for the condom and watched as she brought herself to the first orgasm of the evening.

"You sexy as hell." I ripped the wrapper open, left it on the nightstand and stood.

"You ok?" She asked when I laid her on the bed. I stared at her for a few seconds.

We've been messing around for about seven months now and I found myself wanting to be with her every second of the day and that's not like me. I'm more of a, *let me fuck and I'll see you when I see you,* type of nigga.

"I'm good." I put the condom on and slid in slow. Her pussy was wet as hell and if I'm not careful, I'll cum quick.

"Yea baby just like that. Courage I'm about to.... oh shit..." She succumbed to another one and my ass was in a zone from then on.

I had her in every position possible and right before I let off, I pulled out and nutted on her stomach.

"Why did you pull out?" She asked breathing heavy.

"The condom broke." I removed it and showed her.

"Thank goodness. We not ready for kids." She rolled over and pulled the covers up.

"You damn right." I chuckled and tossed the condom out. I walked back in the room and noticed her upset. What the hell happened that fast?

"What's up?"

"I know we're not a couple and I should've said something about wanting to be more, but how could you?"

"How could I what?"

"You pulled out because the condom broke, and that's fine but you didn't pull outta her?" She turned her phone to me and there was a photo of me leaving the doctor's office with a bitch.

"Drina." I reached out for her.

"Don't touch me." She hopped out the bed and threw a robe on.

"It's been six months now since the two of us being seeing each other; right?" She tightened the belt.

"This photo or should I say, caption under her Instagram photo that she happened to tag me in, says she's only two months."

"Let me talk to you."

"How long have you known?" She asked still visibly upset.

"It doesn't matter." She shook her head.

"It does matter and why didn't you mention having sex with other women when I asked? I wasn't ok with it, but I wasn't stupid either. All you had to do is tell me and I wouldn't have spent so much time with you."

"Drina, she's some chick I messed with off and on."

"Long enough to sleep with her unprotected tho." I put my head down.

"I knew messing with you would hurt. I fucking knew it but I kept telling myself, you're too good to me. You promised to never hurt me and look." She let the tears fall.

"The man I fell in love with has a child on the way and never deemed it necessary to inform the woman he's been with almost every day for the last month." She's right. We've been damn near inseparable these last few weeks.

My mom even knew the difference and asked me to bring over the woman who had all my attention. I planned on telling her to come over the house for dinner one day this week but no need to now.

"I wasn't going to bring it up until after she delivered, and I had a test."

"But in the meantime, you were going to the dr. appointments, satisfying her cravings, and buying things for the child in the process, right?" I remained quiet because I was getting pissed off and she's never seen the other side of me and I'm not tryna show her.

"You know Courage, I thought you were the one. I mean, you are every woman's dream, a Prince Charming, a protector but most of all, you're a disappointment."

"WHAT?" I barked making her jump and move away.

"That's right. Get mad. I don't care." She continued talking shit.

"I told you my darkest secrets Courage and you couldn't even keep it real with me about a woman who's having your child. What, were you scared? Nah, you couldn't have been because your name is Courage." I chuckled and finished putting my sneakers on."

"Don't bother contacting me once you leave. I can't compete with a child and a woman who's already being messy. You can't be trusted, and I refuse to lose sleep over a man who could care less about anyone's feelings but his own." I don't know what came over me, but I had pushed her against the wall. She didn't hit hard but the fact I did it, was a shock.

"You need to go." I let go and threw my shirt on.

"Drina, I didn't mean to..." She put her hand up.

"Please don't. Just go." I walked over to her and she literally ran herself into a wall on the opposite side of the room, just to get away from me. Terror was written on her face and that shit hurt me. Never in a million years did I wanna make her fear me. I left her house and went straight to the source.

BOOM! BOOM!

"Who is it?" Her voice spoke from the other side. I didn't say shit and pushed past her when the door opened.

"What type of stupid bitch doesn't see who's at the door before answering it?"

"No one comes here Rage but you." I instantly became aggravated when she said it because it only proves we are or were more than what I told Andrina.

Ciara used to be my girl for about two years. Last year, she said it was over because I was away too much. I didn't fight her on it. Wasn't a need when she is absolutely correct. I spent a lotta time outta the country and around the world in general. It's who I am, who my family are.

The Waters family owned every hotel, club, shopping malls and car dealerships in Miami. We also owned businesses in Dubai, Italy, Mexico, Paris and England. Some would say were millionaires, but they'd be wrong. We're billionaires who had more money than Bill Gates himself and that's independently.

My father was born into money from his ancestors. He went to college, graduated with a degree in Finance, Accounting and Business. He wanted to make sure he knew the ins and outs of everything. After college, he met my ghetto ass mother, who was attending community college herself for accounting.

Long story short, they linked up and started putting money into stocks which made them even richer. Not trusting anyone with their finances, they handled all their own money and in a matter of ten years, they were multi-millionaires.

My father took that and ran with it. He started buying hotels and eventually almost the entire Miami area. If there's a hot spot in Miami, you can bet we own it.

Our parents refused to allow us to fall victim to the streets and drugs. Therefore; they paid a lot of money to have us attend the prestigious white schools but still took us to the hood to visit my mom's side of the family. He wanted to make sure we knew what it's like to struggle.

Granted, we spent the weekends there and saw and did a lot more than we let our parents know. In my opinion, it's what groomed us into the people we are today. We not hood niggas per say but we damn sure get shit done when need be.

"Explain to me why you tagged Andrina on Instagram?" She pouted and plopped down on the couch.

"Because you're supposed to be with me Rage. I'm pregnant with your child and it's time we start acting like a family."

"I know you joking right now." I had my hands against my mouth as if I were praying to keep myself calm.

"No, I'm not and your mom agrees."

"You called my mother?" She smirked.

"I did and..."

"And nothing." I stood and headed to the door.

"Ciara, you decided to end our relationship; not me. You're the one who didn't wanna stick around."

"Yea but..." I cut her off.

"Yea but now you think because you're pregnant, I'm supposed to stop living my life to cater to you."

"Well yea."

"Well ya sound stupid." I shook my head.

"Rage please."

"You fucked up a relationship I was building with a woman all because we had too much to drink and I forgot to strap up." We had unprotected sex a lot and I always pulled out.

The night in question, I didn't have a condom and it was

spur of the moment sex. Andrina and I weren't having sex yet and a nigga was horny. I should've told her, but Ciara has never been petty or childish to my knowledge until now.

I don't even know how she found out about Andrina. Not that she was a secret because we were always out together, but Ciara never said a word or asked; yet she thought it was necessary to tag her in some photo I didn't even know was being taken.

"Ok so you're not together anymore. Why don't you stay the night and..?"

"Hell no. So you can take more pictures and tag her. I'm good and do me a favor." I turned on my way out the door.

"Don't say shit to her and only contact me if it's about the baby. I'm not talking about cravings for food, sex or anything else. Strictly about the baby." I slammed the door before she could respond. Fuck her.

CHAPTER 6

Conscience 'Cee' Waters

"I'm fine Rock. Just leave me alone." I said to my man of eight months.

"Tha fuck you mean leave you alone?" He followed me around my bedroom as I got dressed to go visit my parents. I hadn't seen them since the fiasco at the sports bar and to be honest, had they not threatened me to come, I'd still be lying down.

"Look. I don't think this relationship is gonna work out. I mean we're from two different worlds and..."

"And what? Huh? You think because your family has money, you better than me? Is that what it is?" My mouth fell open. I've never told him how much we made but he is aware that we have some money. Not that we're the mob or anything but our names do ring bells in the world as far as money makers.

"Julian." I referred to his real name.

"I never said I'm better than you." Rock may not have the type of money I do but he's doing very well for himself. Yea, he's the top drug supplier out here in Miami and all of Florida and there's not a person around who'll fuck with him that I know of.

"Then what's the problem?" I finished getting dressed.

"Your ex is a problem Rock and right now, I don't have the energy to deal with her drama."

Rock and I only been together for eight months and here I am expecting our first child in six. I know how it happened, but I don't know why it did when we were always careful. He claims the condom popped and he didn't realize until we were done. I can't say he's lying, and I can't say he's telling the truth either.

Anyway, he and I met in South Beach at one of my brothers' clubs. He was in VIP, where I was at the bar with my friend Lisa chilling. I had my own section reserved because you never get the feel of a place when you're in one section. Plus, I loved to dance and so did Lisa.

Long story short, he spotted me and sent two bottles of Ace of Spades over. I didn't care for the drink and still offered up my thanks through the waitress. Two hours later, he made his way over to me and we had a quick conversation before exchanging numbers. He said it was too loud to try and get to know one another and I agreed.

Two days later, he took me on a yacht, that I later found out is his, and he wined and dined me. He had a jazz band on board and shockingly, I enjoyed myself. I'm usually an R&B type of chick but this band was good.

As time went on, we became inseparable besides work and now here I am pregnant and dealing with a scorned ex. I understand women can't let go; however, they've been broken up for five years. He said, the bitch is crazy and it's why he got rid of her. They have no kids together, he doesn't pay any of her bills and lastly, the two of them never had sex. I know it's crazy.

How in the hell you bugging over a man you never been sexually active with? When I questioned him on why, he told me, her hygiene wasn't up to par. I asked him nothing else afterwards and left it alone.

Unfortunately, the bitch found out about the pregnancy an stalks me any chance she gets. The day at the sports bar, I was waiting on Lisa. She cancelled at the last minute which pissed me off because Rock's ex and her dirty ass crew came in being ghetto. I had no problem whooping her ass in the parking lot. It took a lot outta me though because of the pregnancy.

I appreciated the heck outta the two women who stepped up to intervene. Come to find out, one of the bitches they beat up, had a knife. I can't imagine what they were gonna do had I been alone.

Rage and his people pulled up, but the bitches jumped in the car and sped off. The two who helped me disappeared. I hadn't seen them to say thank you and had no idea where to look. Rage said he spoke to one at Walgreens but that's as far as it goes. I can't even say I'd remember who they are if I saw them again.

"I told you, I'm gonna handle it."

"You've been saying it and yet here we are still dealing with it." Consequence wanted to handle it and then Rage wanted to after the bar incident. I asked them not to because it would cause an issue between me and Rock. No man wants another to handle his affairs; especially when he's capable of doing it.

"I'm tired of fighting with you over it Rock. Let's just co-parent and stay friends." I could see his fists ball up.

"Bet. This is what you want right?" He ran downstairs and returned with a big black garbage bag.

"What are you doing?"

"This is over right?" He asked pulling out the drawers that held his clothes in it.

"Rock."

"Nah Cee. You tired of dealing with her shit and I get it." He stopped putting things in the bag.

"Did it ever occur to you that I can't control what a bitch says or does?" I didn't say anything.

"I can murk her the minute I leave this house and then what Cee? You'll find another reason on why you don't wanna be with me."

"Rock, I do wanna be with you."

"Really because three weeks ago, you wanted to break up because I didn't answer your call at two in the morning. I call you back, what, 30 seconds later and you say I'm cheating when I'm sitting in front of your house." I remained quiet.

I woke up thinking he was here and when he wasn't, I called him. He didn't answer and at that time of the morning I assumed he's fucking. He called back and sure enough was sitting outside looking for the key.

"Last month, you wanted to break up because I arrived at the doctor's appointment three minutes late. You know I had a business meeting and wasn't gonna be on time, and you still threw a fit." I leaned on the wall with my head tilted back crying.

"Oh, and two months ago, you didn't wanna be bothered because I brought home food and you decided at the last minute, it wasn't what you wanted. So what did you say, I don't follow directions." He slammed the dresser drawer.

"I figured it was your hormones, but nah. At this point, I can't tell if you want a man or a child."

"A child?" I asked.

"Someone you can tell what to do and as you say, follow directions. I'm out." He grabbed his bag and headed down the stairs quickly.

"ROCK!" I shouted and he stopped at the front door.

"I'm sorry."

"Yea a'ight. I'll see you at the next doctor's appointment and I'll try not you be late." I thought the windows would shatter from the way he shut the door.

I took a seat at the top of the stairs and cried my eyes out. I loved Rock but he's right. I did treat him like a kid, and he didn't deserve it. He's been very good to me and despite his ex doing dumb shit, I really had no need to complain.

* * *

"I blame your father." My mom stood in the doorway of her living room. I drove here after getting myself together and been on the couch ever since. I told them what happened, and she's been going on and on about it.

"What you blame me for?" My dad shook his head.

"You spoiled her and so did Consequence and Courage. She's so used to getting her way, she done pushed the best thing that ever happened to her away." I started crying. Like I said, Julian is very good to me and I should've appreciated and treated him better.

"Keep it up Conscience and you gonna be alone forever."

"No she won't because I'll be here." My dad rubbed my arm.

"Awww daddy."

"Daddy my ass. He won't be keeping you warm at night and cuddled up with you. Tomorrow you need to make things right with Rock and if you don't want to, that's fine too. Just don't be one of those ratchet women who get upset when their ex moves on. You know acting all ghetto and shit." She walked in the other room.

"Am I spoiled daddy?"

"Hell yea." Consequence butted in. He must've just gotten here.

"You more spoiled than a kid. Why you asking anyway?" He sat on the couch.

"Julian left her." My mom re-entered the room to tell him. He shook his head.

"Damn sis. He was good for you."

"ALRIGHT DAMN! I GET IT. I'M A BITCH AND DESERVE TO BE ALONE." I shouted and it got quiet in the room.

"Leave it alone Consequence." My father attempted to calm him down. He stood and walked closer to me.

"Who the fuck you yelling at?" I swallowed hard.

"I don't give a shit what you going through. What I do know is you better watch your motherfucking mouth or sister or not, I'll make sure you never open it again. Are we clear?" I nodded and hid my face in my father's chest.

Rage is bad when it comes to anger, but Consequence is on a whole other level. One thing he didn't play no matter who you were; is disrespect. He hated to do it to someone, or for someone to do it to him. He goes by the saying, treat people how you wanna be treated. He doesn't give anyone a pass, not even us.

"Let me go before I beat yo ass. Where's my son?"

"Right here daddy." He came running down the steps with his nanny. She was an older Spanish woman who's been around since we were kids.

"Aunty Cee when are you taking me to the park again?" I glanced over at my brother.

"Answer him. What you looking at me for?" I jumped when he spoke.

"I'll take you Saturday. Be ready by two ok?" He ran over and hugged me.

"Love you lil Con." We shortened his name a long time ago.

"Love you too aunty. Daddy, I'm hungry." He put his hand in my brothers and Consequence gave me the evilest face ever. I tried to ignore it, but he has the ability to scare you with just a look. Thankfully I'm his sister; otherwise he'd probably kill me.

CHAPTER 7

Julian 'Rock' S

"Tell me again why you thought it was ok to fuck with my girl?" I questioned Monica as she sat in a chair with her arms tied behind it.

"I'm sorry Rock. It's just..."

"It just what huh?"

"It's just you never gave us a chance. We were a couple all of two months and you up and bounced." I shook my head.

"We would've never worked because your hygiene is horrible, and your pussy smelled through your pants. I probably would've thrown up if you took them down." She was embarrassed and I didn't care.

"This is gonna be my last time telling you to stay the fuck away from her. And to show you I mean business, I'm gonna leave you with something. Mark bring it here." I said to one of my workers.

I didn't have friends or people I grew up with. I'm kind of a loner because I didn't trust a soul. The only person I did trust is my brother and he passed away from colon cancer two years ago. I took that shit hard too and almost lost everything I had. It wasn't until I ran across Conscience in the club, did shit changed.

That exact night, I had a meeting in my office with a guy named Reg, who I've been supplying for years. He knew about my brothers passing and at first, he refused to deal with the person I left in charge to get myself together. This guy Samuel has been around for five years and I never had an issue. His money was always right, his team was good etc...

Like I said, I didn't really fuck with anyone and since he's been around the longest, I felt he could do it for a few months.

During my grieving process, he contacted me when necessary and to my knowledge, shit was good. It wasn't until Reg hit me up and said the product was skimmed off of and watered down. I never called Samuel and had someone do a pickup just to see if it were true and I'll be damned.

Come to find out Samuel hired a whole new team to do his dirty work. I had one of my loyal workers record it so when I brought it to his attention, the proof is there. I never wanted to be the person to go off hearsay.

The day I called him in, he didn't know but I already disposed of each person he had helping him. Samuel tried to deny it, then he saw the video and started pleading his case. He claims he didn't know and would never steal from me. You know the lies they tell to stay alive.

I murked him right in my office and had his hands sent to

his mother with a letter reading, *never bite the hand who feeds you*. She tried to get the law involved but like any Connect, the law is on my side.

Anyway, it hurt like hell to walk away from Conscience because she was the light at the end of my tunnel. I loved that woman more than I could ever say.

We hit it off well in the beginning and even though she came after my brother's passing, she helped me through my grievance in more ways than one. She was there for some of my darkest days and stayed right beside me. I'll always love her for that and my child she's carrying.

I can't and won't allow her to treat me like shit when I don't even let niggas on the street do it. She knew she was wrong too because she's sent me text messages apologizing, left me voicemails and sent me one of the freaky videos we made to remind me of her. I'll probably go back but she gonna wait until I'm ready.

"Be careful bro." Mark said walking in.

"What... what's that..?" Monica stuttered.

"This my friend, is Lola." She sucked her teeth at the coyote in front of her drooling at the mouth.

"Lola here is a wild animal I had shipped from Arizona." I bent down to pet her.

"Why do you have one?"

"Good question. You see your four friends over there looking half dead?" I pointed to them in the corner.

I paid some hood girls from the projects to whoop their ass after they tried jumping my girl. The chicks I hired, used brass knuckles and steeled toe boots on them and right now, they all fucked up.

"Let us go Rock and I promise not to bother her again."

"I'm gonna let you go but they're not going anywhere." I took the leash from Mark and had him push her in the chair in front of her friends.

"Right now, Mark is throwing dead rabbit and deer meat on these bitches. Lola here and her three friends are gonna find them." She swung her neck at the other three coyotes being brought over.

"Rock don't do this."

"I didn't; you did. You got them mixed up in yo drama and they're gonna know what it's like to fuck with mine." I had three other guys bring the other coyotes over. Each guy had to hold one separate because they were hungry and struggling to get to the food.

"Pay attention Monica because your death, may be a hundred times worse." I nodded and all of us let go. Those coyotes were ripping those bitches to shreds. Monica started to vomit and then dry heave.

"Let's go." After the coyotes finished, I gripped her arm and led her out the door. This warehouse is humongous, and no one knew where it was, so I wasn't concerned about her seeing anything.

"If you even look at my girl wrong again, I'm gonna kill you." She took a deep breath when a black van pulled up.

"We good?" Rage asked when he stepped out. Yea, I rock with Conscience brothers.

We've known one another a lot longer than I've known their sister but only on a business level. They weren't into drugs, but their kill game is on some serial killer, torture type, cannibal, crazy shit. I thought people were terrified of me, but they are terrified of Consequence and Rage and with those names, they should be.

"One last thing Monica." She turned around.

"I know you don't think you getting off that easy." I told her.

"I need to smoke. Please let me go." I shook my head. Monica had an obsession with getting high.

I had no idea at first because she moved here from Houston. Her appearance was on point and she had good conversation. It wasn't until two months into us being in a relationship, did I smell her. I assumed it smelled because she was sweating or something. It's gets hot as hell out here.

Sadly, the smell started to become a stench and it's when I realized the tracks in her arms. She's brown skin so you'd only notice them if you're looking. I asked if she's a user and she said occasionally. I left her alone right away and even sent her to rehab three times. She left the rehab each time, so I washed my hands with her. I could've remained cordial with her, but she blew it fucking with Conscience.

"Smoke on this." I jammed my gun in her mouth and pulled the trigger. Her brains were everywhere. There wasn't a need to keep her around. Rage and I spoke about some business and parted ways. At least that's handled.

* * *

"I'm sorry Julian." I turned to see Conscience standing there glowing. We were at the doctor's office and I beat her here.

"Sorry for what?" I pretended to be more interested in my phone.

"The way I speak to you. You're my man and not my child. You treat me very well and... and..." I looked up and she was crying.

"And what?" I rose to my feet.

"And I love you. I'm tired of sleeping alone. If you wanna sleep in the other room I don't care. Just don't leave me." I wiped the tears.

"This baby got my hormones acting up, but it doesn't give me the right to treat you like shit. I'm so sorry baby."

"We'll be right back." I told the nurse who paid more attention to us then the woman in front of her.

"Stop crying." I turned the water on and locked the door.

"I can't help it. I..." I cut her off by intertwining our tongues and pulling down the leggings she wore, along with her panties.

"I'm only gonna be a minute and you pregnant already so we good." She nodded. We were both breathing heavily and rushing to get my jeans and boxers down.

"Got damn I missed this." She was soaking wet and my nut rushed to the tip. I took my dick out and tapped it on her clit.

"I'm about to cum baby. Oh shit." She whispered.

"Me too." I entered her again and the two of us exploded.

"You ok?" I asked kissing her neck.

"Yes. I just wanna sleep." I laughed.

"After the appointment."

"Ok." I let her down and wiped the two of us up. We stepped out the bathroom and no one said a word. I didn't care if they did. We took a seat and waited for them to call us.

Afterwards, I drove to her house, fucked the shit outta her and fell asleep. I hadn't slept well since we broke up. I'm about to be in la la land.

CHAPTER 8
Consequence

"**A**re you going to find me a mommy?" I almost choked on the French fry. Me and my son were at the Dolphin Mall eating in the Cheesecake Factory for lunch.

I stared at my son and wanted to beat his mother's ass just because she left. So what I told her not to ever come around me; the bitch knew where my parents lived and could've stopped by. I would've given the bitch a pass if it meant my son could have a mother.

"Why you need a mother when you have nana, aunty Cee and Alma?" I placed another fry in my mouth.

"They're not my mommy. I want a mom. Can you find me one?" I lifted his head up.

"It takes a while to know a woman, but I promise when she comes around, you'll be the first one she meets."

"Make it soon daddy. I want her there for my graduation."

"Well graduation is a long time away." At least, I had time.

"No dad. My kindergarten graduation."

"Son, I can't find you no mommy quick like that?"

"Why not? Aunty Cee found uncle Rock. Uncle Rage found Ciara and she's about to have my cousin."

"For you to be five years old, you damn sure know a lot. I told them to stop talking around you." I shook my head laughing.

"They don't know I be listening." I told him to finish his food so we could go. Foot Action hit my line and mentioned they had the new Jordan's I ordered. I wanted to pick them up and some new outfits for Lil C. It was early October and it gets chilly in these fake ass winter months. I'll take this over other areas though.

"Thank you and please come again." The woman said smiling.

"Before you try and flirt, make sure your teeth are pearly white and there's nothing green in between." She instantly covered her mouth.

"Girl, I told you not to speak. He mean as fuck every time he comes in here." I winked at the young girl who always waited on us. She's the only one I trusted with our food, which is why I always called before coming and requested to be seated in her area.

"I try and tell them Mr. Waters, but they don't listen." I handed her a tip and headed into the store.

"Yo. Consequence, what's good?" The guy Eric said. He worked here and always put me down for the new Jordan's. I wasn't signing up for no damn lottery. In return, I compensated him with money or VIP at the club. I can't front; he gives me mad discounts too.

"Shit. You got the sneakers?"

"Yea." I walked behind him.

"Look, I have this new Jordan outfit for lil man too."

"It better be fly."

"Don't play me Consequence. Lil C like my cousin and we gotta stay fly for the ladies. Ain't that right?" He gave my son a pound and stepped in the back room.

I walked over to the kid section and a smell invaded my nostrils. It was female and the scent was intoxicating. I never smelled anything like it on a woman. I turned to see who she was an only caught the backside of the chick.

Shorty had on some fitted jeans; showing off her slightly plump ass. Not those humongous one's bitches are getting. Her hair was to the middle of her back and each time she bent down to try on a different sneaker, her scent crossed my nose. I wanted to ask her name but that's not my style. Women come to me and ain't shit about to change.

I'm slightly conceited and I blame it on the women. I wouldn't consider myself ugly and I damn sure can dress. I'm every woman's dream even if she doesn't know it.

"Here you go." He handed me the stuff and smiled looking at the woman.

"She bad ain't she?" Eric said basically eye fucking her.

"She hasn't turned around so I can't agree. This outfit fire tho." I laid it on the bench next to my son who was playing on the phone with a pair of beats on his ear as usual.

"Excuse me." The second she opened her mouth; I sucked my teeth. My back was now turned so she couldn't see me.

"What's up sexy?" Eric responded.

"Do you have these in..." I put my foot down after trying on the sneaker and our eyes met. I couldn't tell if she were nervous or about to talk shit.

"Never mind. I'll return when no one is here."

"Man, stop being childish and let him help you. I swear bitches..."

"Bitch?" Her hands were on her hip.

"I'm starting to think you like me fucking you up."

"Y'all know one another?" Eric asked.

"You can say that." She sassed.

"Oh you know me?" I walked up on her.

"What's my name? Where I live? What's my dick size?" I towered over her short self.

"Why do I even bother?" She put her hands up in surrender and backed away.

"Yea, why do you? How you out here shopping anyway when yo ass suspended from work?" I did that shit on purpose and laughed when she stormed out the hotel. That's my shit and she gonna respect me, whether she wants to or not.

"Don't worry about what the fuck I'm doing out here. That's your problem now. Worrying about me." Eric stepped in the middle of us.

"Nah Eric. Let her keep talking." I moved him over and

now our bodies were so close, one more inch and my dick would be touching her chin.

"You need some dick in your life obviously which is why you're acting out. I can't help you though." I let my tongue roam over my bottom lip because now that I see her outside of work and Walmart, she's looking pretty good.

"I wouldn't fuck you with another bitch pussy. And your dick probably small which is why you're so mean. I bet you can't fuck either with yo little dick ass." She picked her things up.

"Keep talking shit and I may let you find out, right before I slice your throat." I whispered in her ear. I could see the goosebumps forming on her arms.

"Yea, you wanna fuck but it'll be a cold day in hell before I stick my dick in you. Now beat it." I brushed past her and put the sneakers in the box to pay for.

"Miss, I'm not sure who you are but can you please just go?" Eric pleaded.

"Why do I have to go?"

"Listen, I'm not tryna sugar coat shit. That nigga crazy and ain't too shy of being a manic. If you value your life, from here on out don't say shit to him. He may be allowing you to bounce now but don't expect him to do it again."

"Ughhhhhh. He makes me sick." She stormed out and almost knocked over a shirt rack.

"Why you save her?" I asked at the register.

"Man, I don't need no one questioning me on why she

died. I'm good." I busted out laughing and grabbed my stuff. I looked around and noticed my son was missing.

"Yo. Where lil C?"

"He was just right there?" He pointed to the spot we were at.

"Fuck!" I ran out the store and stopped short when the same bitch was kneeling in front of him wiping his eyes.

"Tha fuck you do to my son?" I pushed her out the way; making her fall over.

"Nigga, you gonna stop putting your hands on me."

"You ok? What happened? You know better than to leave the store without a grown up." He never walked away from us. I always told him the amount of danger kids put themselves in walking away.

"Some man grabbed me by the shirt and drug me out the store. I started yelling stranger danger out here and the lady you pushed, punched him in the face and he left." I turned my head to see her fixing her clothes.

"Where is he?" I glanced around the area.

"I don't know daddy."

"Why didn't you yell in the store?" I asked.

"The man showed me a small black gun. He said if I made a noise, he would shoot me." I lifted him in my arms and went to the chick who had fear on her face and started walking backwards.

"Stop moving."

"Why? So you can push me again? No thanks." She turned

and before she could leave, I reached out and grabbed the back of her shirt.

"I think God is testing me." She said laughing.

"He ain't testing shit. Shut yo dumb ass up and stop." She snatched away from me.

"I wanted to say thank you for saving my son but it's your fault."

"My fault?" She seemed offended.

"Had you not engaged me in a conversation, this would've never happened."

"Conversation? You know what? I'm not even about to argue. Are you ok sweetie?" He nodded and leaned down to kiss her cheek.

"Now that's how you treat a woman." She kissed him back.

"Whatever. Here." I tried to hand her some money.

"I don't need to be paid for keeping him safe. And the man you're looking for is light skin with a faded haircut. He had a goatee and a medium build. He reminded me of one your guards from Walmart."

"Ron?" I asked.

"Not the one who pushed me too, which by the way I still need an X-ray of my tailbone. Matter of fact, my whole back since you continuously throw me against walls." She put one hand on her hip and leaned to the side.

"You better use that Obamacare and go to the ER."

"I have never in my life met anyone like you. Who the hell raised you?" She turned her mouth up.

"What the fuck eva. Finish giving me details." She pulled her phone out.

"This is him."

"How the fuck am I supposed to see that? The shit mad blurry and it's only his side." I handed the phone back to her.

"I tried to take it quick, but he ran off." She sucked her teeth.

"I can't with you. I'm happy you're ok." She started to walk away.

"CAN YOU BE MY MOMMY?" Shorty stopped.

"Lil Con, what the hell is wrong with you? I told you I'd find one."

"Umm." She was at a loss for words.

"Don't say shit. Just keep walking. I'll deal with this." The chick nodded and walked off. I had to find someone quick because my son is desperate for a mother. I could kill Lauren.

CHAPTER 9
Zakiya

It broke my heart to hear the little boy ask me to be his mother the other day. It made me wonder where his real mom is. Of course, I couldn't ask questions, not that I wanted to with his mean ass father, but I did wanna give him a hug. He's such a handsome kid and you can tell his father dresses him. The little Jordan's on his feet and outfit to match was adorable. I couldn't wait to have a kid.

"Welcome back Miss Zakiya." Jerry said and gestured for me to enter her office. I searched the lobby to make sure that asshole wasn't around.

"Have a seat." She pointed to the chair and sat across from me.

"First let me say, I apologize for having to suspend you."

"It's fine. You were doing your job and to be honest, I needed that time off."

"I guess Andrina did too." She pursed her lips up making me laugh.

"I can't help she doesn't wanna work without me." She shook her head.

"I called you in here because..."

KNOCK! KNOCK!

"One second."

"Here's the paperwork you asked for and congratulations Zakiya." Jerry shook her head no. I was confused.

"What's she talking about?" She opened the folder and passed me an envelope.

"I need you to fill the paperwork out and this will be the key to your new office. Your parking space is close to the employee entrance and you now have the weekends off. Oh, you're getting a $10 raise. Your rate of pay used to be $8 an hour and now it's $18." My mouth was on the floor.

"Congratulations on becoming the manager of housekeeping." She smiled.

"Say what?" She leaned on the desk.

"I don't know what or who you did on your two-week suspension..."

"No you didn't just say that."

"Hey, whatever floats your boat. Anyway, all this came over this morning and I was told to inform you right away." She handed me all the stuff.

"This is crazy. There's not even a manager position open here. And an office? What's going on?"

"Bitch, I have no idea. Take the position and keep your mouth shut on how much you make."

"Jerry, I feel like this is a trick."

"Listen, whoever made this possible will make themselves known soon. People don't do shit for no reason, and you know they'll want to be thanked. Let's go check out your office." I sat there for a few minutes in awe. Who the heck would do this for me?

"Hey boo. Where you going?" Drina asked walking to punch in.

"Evidently, to my new office."

"Office? Bitch when did that happen?" Drina was shocked too.

"Just now and before you ask, I don't know why."

"Well hold on. The bestie has to punch in and come see." I laughed and we waited for her to put her things down. Jerry pressed the button to the elevator and pushed in the number 11.

The eleventh floor held offices, three conference rooms and a whole area for food. This area too could only be accessed if you worked here or stayed on the twelfth floor and up.

"I swear this is the best floor." Andrina said walking behind me.

"Here's your office." I stared at the two steel doors and held my breath in. If the office is as nice as the floor itself, I'll be happy.

"DAMN BITCH! This is nicer than mine." I stood there and glanced around the room.

It held a big beautiful cherry wood desk, with a computer, and iPad sitting on it. There was a television hanging on the wall, along with a small mini bar and a private bathroom. I'm definitely thankful for that. A small refrigerator sat in the corner and so did a loveseat.

The best part of this room was the view outside the huge windows. You could see all of Miami from here. The view is better at the very top, but this is just as good.

"What's this?" Drina asked after moving the chair. I took the bag out her hand and opened it up to find the exact pair of sneakers I wanted in Foot Action.

"No way!" I whispered.

"Who the hell brought you sneakers?" Jerry questioned.

"No idea." I didn't wanna say in case it wasn't him. What am I saying? It had to be him.

"Ok bitch. Tell me what's going on?" Drina said handing me an envelope out the drawer and one rose.

"I really don't know." Jerry's phone rang and she took the call outside the office.

"Are you sure?"

"Positive." I took a seat in the chair and opened the envelope. There was a thank you card, and it had a saying but what he wrote sounded better.

"I wanted to say thank you again for keeping my son safe, even though it's your fault he was taken. (LOL) Seriously, I appreciate it from the bottom of my heart. In return, I had to compensate

you and since you refuse money, this is what you'll get. Thank you again. Consequence."

"Consequence. So that's your name?" I whispered and laid my head back on the chair with the card against my chest.

"Let me find out you gave the pussy to your dirty landlord again."

"Bitch, you tried it." I rolled my eyes and put the card in the front of my smock.

I wasn't ashamed for sleeping with the manager of the apartments I stayed in. Money has always been tight and since I had no kids, the state wouldn't help. My light bill was due and fuck it, I wanted some nice furniture. He paid me to fuck and I used it to my advantage. It only happened five maybe six times, but I made enough to get what I needed.

"Who did this for you then?" We were staring out the window.

"I did." Both of us turned and I couldn't help but get turned on again. He was so sexy, and his presence screamed respect, even though I had a hard time giving it to him.

"Damn bitch. You did not tell me you hooked up with the guy who put his hands on you." She smirked. I pushed her on the side.

"Why did you do this?" I waved my hand around.

"Can you give us a minute?"

"Not if you're gonna hit her. We may not be able to beat

you, but we'll jump you in here." He chuckled and I squeezed my legs tight. What is this man doing to me?

"It's ok Drina." Our eyes never left each other.

"Before you could jump me, her throat would be slit, and you'll be hanging upside down with your guts hanging out. Have a good day." He said and closed the door.

"Must you be violent?"

"It's a habit. Do you like your office?" He walked over to me.

"It's very nice but you didn't have to do this."

"You're right I didn't. However; my mother said, and I quote, *"you better compensate her for saving my grand baby. Matter of fact, bring her over here."*

"So this is a ploy to get me over your mothers?" He shrugged.

"You could've just asked."

"Would you have said yes?"

"Probably not? Being around you makes me wanna fight all the time." He chuckled and his eyes roamed my body. It made me very uncomfortable.

"It's not many women who can talk shit to me and live to tell the story." He leaned on the wall next to me.

"Why am I special?"

"I don't know. Shit, I was fucking this bitch last night and you were the only one on my mind. That shit has never happened to me." I blushed.

"I don't know what you blushing for. I damn near killed the bitch when I put my hand around her throat."

"Does your mom know you speak this way?"

"She's worse than me."

"I don't need to meet her then." He started laughing.

"I'm serious. You've been on my mind a lot and not in a good way. But after you kept my son safe, I had to call a truce. You could've kept going and instead, put yourself in danger and I respect that."

"It's ok Consequence."

"From here on out, I'll try not to fuck with you." I gave him the side eye.

"Are you going to give it a 100% try or just 50?"

"Not sure. It depends on you and your attitude." I sucked my teeth.

"See, you need to learn how to tone it down." He used his two fingers to turn my face to his.

"Every action doesn't need a reaction. Remember that." At that very moment, neither of us moved. We were lost in one another. He brought his face down to me and placed his soft and juicy lips on mine. He didn't even use tongue and I came on myself.

"If I didn't wanna kill you, I'd probably fuck you all over this office."

"Gee thanks." He pushed me gently against the window and both of his hands were now over my head as he stared down at me.

"You are sexy, ain't no mistaken that. You're just not ready for a nigga like me." I wanted to scream out *yes I am* but he's probably right.

"I'll make it so you never even think about another man, on top of fucking your whole world up." He ran his fingertips down my arm.

"What's the name of your perfume?" He smelled my neck.

"Hypnose."

"I've never smelled anything like it. Wear it to my mom's place and I may give you the dick." He pressed his lips on mine and still never stuck is tongue in.

"I'm not sure I want it." He licked his lips.

"Even you don't believe that." He backed away smirking.

"I'll pick you up tomorrow around seven." He opened the door.

"Wait! I didn't give you my address."

"Like I said, I'll pick you up around seven. Oh, someone will be here to help you get situated in your new position." He winked and stepped out.

"About time. Got my new boss looking crazy." Drina said walking in.

"What happened?"

"Ugh, I have a date to meet his mom tomorrow."

"Bitchhhhhhh."

"It's because I saved his son." I told her what happened, and she agreed. They probably all wanted to thank me. Whatever the case, I guess it couldn't hurt being in his presence again.

CHAPTER 10

Consequence

"**I** WANNA KNOW WHO THE FUCK TRIED TO TAKE MY SON!" I shouted at the two men who sat in front of me barely breathing.

Ron wasn't with me when Lil Con was almost taken. However; I still had people in the parking lot.

After I got in my car, I noticed two trucks speeding out. I couldn't dare chase with my son. I had my guys follow them and unfortunately, one vehicle got away. It had to be the guy who attempted to abduct lil Con because these black mother-fuckers didn't resemble shit like the photo.

"It wasn't us."

"Obviously." I walked closer to the two ropes hanging down and made sure they were tight around the block.

"Bring those two cinderblocks over." Ron did like I asked and placed them under the ropes.

"This is what's gonna happen." I lifted one of the dudes up, walked him to the rope and stood him on the block. John did the same with the other. Neither of these men had shoes or socks on which is going to make this even more comical.

"I'm gonna tie this rope around your neck as you stand on this block. I need some questions answered and each one you get wrong, the rope will lift, removing you from the block."

"We don't know nothing."

"We don't know nothing." I mocked him and tightened the rope on both men. John was at one end holding it to lift and Ron had the other.

"First question... How long has someone been watching me or should I say my son?" I stared to see who would answer first.

"I don't know." I nodded and the rope was lifted a little.

"Second... Where does the person live who tried to take my son?" No one spoke. The guys lifted the rope more.

"Once the rope is high enough you will be standing on your tippy toes. You're going to try and save yourself because it's a reaction but remember, fidgeting around can make the block tip over and then what?" I shrugged.

"Please. All I know is, some guy from outta town is here and doesn't care for your family. He said, the child is your pride and joy so take him at the first chance. We were only there to make sure you didn't catch him." One of the men said. I made my way to him and kicked the cinderblock over. His neck snapped instantly.

"If you wanna get this rope from around your neck, I suggest you tell me what I need to know."

"Ok. Ok. He lives out in Tampa with his wife. She owns a

beauty salon and his mom works at the grocery store. We were all tryna make money to leave Florida. I swear man, that's all I know."

"The name of the salon and what's his girls name?" As he gave me the information, I had Ron let the rope down and removed it from around his neck.

"How do you wanna die?"

"You said…"

"I said I'd take the rope from around your neck. I never said I wouldn't kill you."

"Please. I gave you all the answers."

"You gave me everything but the one in charges name."

"All I know is he said, you have something that belongs to him and he wants it back." I had no clue what he's talking about because I'm not into the street life. Yea, I take lives if you fuck with me but handling drugs and all that, Nah. I'm legit.

"I don't owe nobody shit." I swung the machete and watched his head roll on the other side of the room.

"Who you owe nigga?" Ron joked.

"I have never borrowed or stolen from anyone, so I have no idea what he's talking about." I dropped the machete.

"Ron, I want you and John to keep an eye on your security. The chick said dude reminded her of someone from Walmart."

"Walmart?" Ron questioned.

"Yea, the day I almost beat the bitch ass because she couldn't wait to come down the aisle."

"Oh yea, I remember." Ron said and started laughing.

"Pay attention to who runs late? Who doesn't have shit to

lose? Have any of them ever discussed not caring for me or my family? Find out who the fuck it is, and we'll find out who's behind this shit."

"We got you boss and don't worry, no one is gonna get lil man." I removed the gloves from my hand, grabbed my keys and left. I still had to get ready to take this chick to my mom's house.

* * *

"Who is it?" Zakiya yelled from behind the door. I continued pecking away on my phone.

"Is that Mr. Consequence?" I saw a few kids on bikes and gave them a head nod. I knew some from lil Con playing football. He did Pop Warner and I took him to practice at the field sometimes and other kids would be there too.

"You could've said who you were." She snatched the door opened and I admired her ass in the jeans as she walked away

Her shirt had a tad bit of cleavage showing but not enough to say it's too much. Her hair was in a ponytail and she slipped on a pair of all black Jordan's. The same ones I purchased for her at Foot Action.

When we parted ways that day, I took my son straight to the car just in case whoever tried to snatch him was waiting. I called Eric and told him to put the sneakers up for me and I'd get them later.

I was angrier with myself for not bringing Ron. He's always with me but sometimes I wanted alone time with Lil Con. It's fucked up someone tried to take him, and had I not been arguing with this chick, it wouldn't have happened. Then again, my son said he had a gun so who knows?

"Who visiting you here?" I observed her apartment and it was neat and clean. The furniture is decent and there were young pictures of her in cheerleading and basketball outfits. I noticed a very old photo with an older woman and man.

"Is this your mom and dad?"

"Yes and no." I gave her a confused look.

"Yes and no?"

"Yes, she's my mom and no he's not my dad. He's my stepfather."

"They stay here with you?"

"No." She had a sad look.

"Your mom is having a hard time getting clean and your stepdad loves the hell outta you." I told her.

"How the hell...?"

"I know a lot more than you think." I waited for her to lock the door.

"This you?"

"Who the fuck else in these projects gonna have a Bentley?" She rolled her eyes.

"I'm just saying? Look around Zakiya. All you see is Hyundai's, Honda's and Toyota's."

"There's a Phantom." I looked and saw Rock inside. I knew it was his because it's only a few in this area and he has one. I wasn't gonna say a word because he does business here and to my knowledge, him and Cee are over. I'd be surprised if he's messing with someone from here tho. That's a big downgrade from my sister.

"Get in." She stopped and stared at me.

"Tha fuck you waiting for?"

"I'm just shocked you opened it for me."

"Despite what you may see, I am a gentleman. Plus, you better tell my mom I did." She shook her head. I closed the door and walked around the other side.

"And you have a driver? What kind of work did you say you do?"

"I didn't." I closed the door and let the driver know we were going to my parents.

On the way, shorty kept staring out the window and then back at me. I laughed on the inside because she could pretend all she wanted but I know she's interested.

"Wow! This is your parents' house? I can't imagine what yours look like." She was amazed and she should be. We are well off and our living quarters are nice as fuck.

"Don't because you'll never see it." She swung her neck.

"You can see my house, but I can't see yours?"

"You in the hood Zakiya. Everyone has seen your house." I shrugged and stepped out.

"I don't need you to open the door." She had an attitude.

"Why you mad now?"

"Because you were being nice for a few minutes and..." She pouted.

"And no one told you to get used to it. That's your fault." She shook her head.

"After tonight, don't talk to me anymore."

"Ok."

SMACK! Her hand went straight to her butt.

"Pussy probably wet as hell right now."

"Just open the door." I did and pushed her in.

"If I didn't think you'd hit me back, I'd smack you."

"At least you're smart. Let's go." I walked ahead of her and everyone was sitting in the living room. They stopped speaking when they saw us.

"Zakiya, this is my mom, my pops, my brother Rage, his annoying ass ex who claims to be pregnant by him, but that's debatable." She shook her head.

"What? Shit we don't know where she been." I led her over to the loveseat.

"Anyway, this is my sons' nanny, Alma who's basically family and you know lil Con." He jumped up when he saw her.

"Dad, you made her my mom. I thought you said it takes time." My son ran and sat on her lap.

"Hi sweetie. I'm not going to be your mom but if you want, we can be friends."

"For now. When you become my mom, I want you to tuck me in at night and take me to school in the morning."

"Bossy huh?"

"My dad said you have to be in order to get stuff done." She looked up at me and I smirked.

"Tha fuck you here for?" I barked at the bitch walking in. She stared at Zakiya and I knew it was gonna be a hectic evening.

CHAPTER 11

Conscience

"**W**hy the fuck you here?" My brother asked Lisa.

"Zakiya, why don't you come in the kitchen with me? Let's get to know one another." My mom said. Her, Zakiya, Alma and my nephew followed behind. Lisa stared her up and down.

It's no secret my brother slept with her and has for years. To my knowledge, he stopped after he got married but once he made Lauren bounce, they were back at it. I told her not to because he's not gonna wife her up, but she didn't listen and started falling for him all over again.

"I had her come over. I didn't know it would be a problem." I told him.

"Yea Consequence, what's the issue?" Lisa said and I swung my neck to look. If she thinks for one second he won't snap on her, she's sadly mistaken.

"Isn't she the woman from Walmart?" I asked moving into the living room.

"Walmart? You mean the bitch you pulled a gun on?" Consequence and Rage both gave her a look.

"I'm just saying. Since when you bring home bitches from the store?" She plopped down on the couch.

"Consequence, she's the woman who helped me when those chicks tried to jump me."

"I knew she looked familiar." Rage chimed in.

"Oh, when this bitch stood you up." Lisa's facial expression changed.

"Son lets go have a smoke." My father knew Consequence was about to snap and smoking would calm him a little.

"Why you keep fucking with him?" I stood next the couch her and Ciara were on.

"You have no idea how good the dick gonna be tonight."

"If he gives you any. You see how he stared at the chick? You gonna have competition boo." Ciara sassed and went in the kitchen.

"Please. The bitch looks broke and who comes for a dinner in sneakers? That ghetto trash don't have shit on me." Lisa said.

"If she don't; why you mad?" I left her sitting there and made my way in the kitchen too.

I noticed how my nephew sat on the Zakiya chicks lap and I think my mom and Alma did as well. Lisa has been around for a long time and he's never grew a bond with her. I don't even think he speaks to Lisa and my rude brother isn't gonna say anything because he could care less.

"Zakiya?" I spoke and she turned to me.

"Thanks for having my back at the sports bar. I didn't plan on fighting and damn sure didn't know they were gonna jump me; so thank you."

"To be honest, I wasn't gonna help at all." Consequence stepped in as she said it.

"Why is that?"

"I think you know why but I'll say it. You pulled a gun on my friend at the store. Why would I help someone I didn't know and I damn sure wasn't gonna help someone who did that."

"Why did you?" My mom asked.

"My friend said it wouldn't be right to let anyone jump a pregnant woman."

"So you knew who she was and still helped? I'd say that's a good thing." Alma chimed in.

"I guess. Are you still pregnant? You didn't lose it fighting the other chick; did you?"

"Not at all and regardless of the reason you came to my aide; I'm appreciative." She nodded.

"Ok everyone. Dinner is ready. Ladies can you help me bring the food out?" My mom asked and all of us stood. The men went in the dining room and took lil Con with them.

"This is Consequence's favorite, so I'll take it." She snatched the greens out Zakiya's hand.

"Umm. Ok. I'm not sure why you're bugging because it's a bowl for everyone to eat out of but go off boo." I busted out laughing.

"I'll have you know Miss ghetto thing that Consequence doesn't do hood."

"Then what you worried about?" Zakiya took the biscuits off the counter and sashayed passed Lisa.

"This is gonna be fun." Ciara joked as we all picked the different platters up. My mom said grace and she always made sure lil Con ate first.

We sat around the table talking about my pregnancy and I was surprised to hear Zakiya join in. She wanted to have children of her own one day and hoped to buy a house as well. It took us by surprise because even though we as family know where she's from, it didn't stop her from wanting better. Most people were comfortable receiving assistance. She wanted more outta life and I could respect her hustle.

"Zakiya, you and Consequence have been bumping into one another a lot lately. You sure you're not stalking him?" I almost spit my food out. Lisa was tryna get a rise outta this woman. I could see my brothers face turn up.

"Stalking? Not at all. If anything, I try and stay away from him."

"Hmph."

"He is probably the most ignorant, arrogant, conceited and rude man I've ever met. If he didn't mention his parents wanting to meet me, I would've never been here."

"Y'all wanted to meet her?" Lisa became offended.

"Oh, they didn't do the same for you. That's a shame." Consequence laughed and so did everyone else.

"Anyway, no fear Lisa. You won't see me again; right Consequence? This is a one-time thing." She smiled and put a forkful of greens in her mouth.

As dinner went on, conversations flowed until the dessert came out. My mom made her favorite key lime pie and chocolate cake. I couldn't wait to sink my teeth into it.

"Are you coming over later?" Lisa asked my brother casually and his facial expression said a lot, even if no words left his mouth.

"Miss Zakiya. Can you come see my room?" Lil Con had finished and didn't want dessert. He was too excited to show Miss Zakiya everything.

"You have a room here?"

"I have a room everywhere I go. When you become my mom, I'll have one at your house if you and daddy don't live together." I almost used the bathroom on myself as I watched Lisa's face change.

"Let's go see your room. Mr. and Mrs. Waters, do you mind?"

"Absolutely not. Have at it but be careful. He has Legos everywhere." She wiped her mouth and stood.

All of us; including Lisa watched Consequence stare at the two of them. This is the first woman he's brought here since the bitch Lauren left. It's crazy to see how intrigued he is by Zakiya. It's weirder to see how much my nephew clung to her right away.

"Say what you need to say before Zakiya returns Lisa because if you come for her one more time, I'ma fuck you up." My brother said in a firm tone.

"Babe, I..."

"Babe? Bitch are you crazy calling me that?" None of us said a word. We're used to him treating her like trash. Hell, if she like it, we love it.

"I just wanted to know if you're coming over?" He had his elbows on the table with his fist under his chin. Some would think he was thinking, but he's trying hard to calm himself down.

"You my woman Lisa?"

"Consequence?"

"Answer the question." He turned to her.

"Are you my woman?"

"No." She put her head down.

"Exactly. Stop acting like we more than what we are. I told you this before. Now if you want me to come by and fuck you; I will. However; you should know Zakiya will be on my mind. If you ok with that, then I'll slide through."

"Consequence?" We all turned to see Zakiya looking embarrassed.

"I didn't come here to start any problems."

"Too late for that." Lisa spoke low but we all heard her.

"You good. What's up?"

"Nothing. It's getting late and I have to work tomorrow."

"I hardly call changing people's sheets and blankets working." Lisa just couldn't shut up. Zakiya took the hoop earrings off and called Lisa outside.

"I apologize Mr. and Mrs. Waters, but she been asking for

this ass whooping all night. Meet me outside." Zakiya went to the door and we all turned to Lisa.

"What?" Lisa asked as if she didn't know we were waiting for her to fight Zakiya.

"Aren't you gonna meet her outside?" My mom asked.

"Never allow a woman to offer you to a fight and sit there. Go show her she's not taking Consequence from you." My mom was hysterical laughing as Lisa sat there.

"What you waiting for?" Zakiya asked. All of us turned back to the door and Zakiya was ready.

"I'm not about to fight over him."

"Nah. You not about to get yo ass whooped in front of him. That's the problem. Stupid ass bitch."

"A'ight Zakiya. Ma, I'll be back to pick up Lil Con." My brother stood.

"Your driver can take her home." Lisa snapped.

"I want Consequence to take me home. He's looking delicious tonight and I think, it's time to channel the sexual chemistry between us." Consequence walked straight up to Zakiya and kissed her.

"He's never kissed me in all these years. What the fuck?"

"That should tell you something." Alma said laughing.

"Let me see what that pussy can do." He patted her on the ass and shut the door. Rage was cracking up and my father just shook his head.

"Let's get this cleaned up." We started helping my mom when Rock stopped by.

"Hey babe. I stayed at work late because I thought you weren't coming." He always came to the dinners.

"I wasn't but Consequence brought the chick Zakiya, who saved lil Con and he wanted us all to meet her."

"Zakiya?" I looked at him.

"You know her?" He paused for a few seconds.

"Nah." Something was off with the way he responded but I left it alone. If Consequence and her get together, I'm sure he'll see her and I'll go from there.

"Don't think too hard babe. I don't want no one but you." He wrapped his arms around my waist and leaned down to kiss me.

"Better not or I promise not to do those special things in the bedroom."

"Lies you tell." I started laughing.

"I love you Julian."

"I love you too and don't ever become uncomfortable or intimidated around no woman I used to be with. She's the past for a reason."

"So you know Zakiya?"

"I'm saying in general. Don't think another woman will ever take your place. We belong together." Funny how he didn't respond.

"Yes we do." I had him grab his plate out the kitchen and we drove to my house together. Lisa brought me anyway.

CHAPTER 12

Zakiya

"Sorry about what happened at your parents. She kept pushing me." I said to Consequence on the ride back to my house.

"It's all good. She deserved it and we both know it." He put the phone down.

"So, you sucking me off in the house or what?"

"Nigga what?" I snapped.

"I can pay if that's what you want." I mushed him and felt my body being pressed to against the door.

"You want me to break this shit?"

"No." I was scared to death.

"Then keep your hands to yourself." He let go.

"I asked because you fuck for money, right?" I rubbed my wrist.

"Consequence please don't say anything else to me. You can

have that position at the job, and I'll work elsewhere. After you drop me off, forget you ever met me." I felt the tears tryna to escape.

"I'm just saying. The manager of your building said..." I snapped my neck to look at him.

"What?"

"The first day I saw you, I found out all your information. I came through and asked where you lived. The guy claimed to be the person running the complex and informed me of how you make money. I figured it's why you said that shit at the house." I was shocked.

"My question to you is, are you fucking me for free, or do I need to stop at an ATM?" All I could do is burst into tears.

"Don't let those salty ass things hit my seat." I wiped them as fast as they could come. This Bentley is nice as hell. He parked in front of my building and parked.

"Thanks for the dinner and the ride home. Have a nice life." I picked my things up and walked to my apartment. He pulled off and I let the tears fall again.

He was so nice tonight; what happened? He opened the car door for me, had decent conversations with me at the table, even made sure I wasn't uncomfortable and kept asking if I were good. I thought everything went well and then, this happened.

I stripped outta my clothes and rushed to get in the shower. I felt dirty being around him and then, he mentioned how I slept with the property manager. The way it came out his mouth, it sounded like I was a prostitute or something. At least, I don't have to be bothered with him again.

I stepped in my room and almost jumped out my skin.

"How did you get in here?"

"I have a key." He lifted it up and I tried to snatch it.

"Why are you here and I'm not a prostitute?" He removed the towel and stared at my body. I wasn't ashamed or nervous; just confused on why he's here and looking at me naked.

"I know you're not, which is why I cut that niggas tongue out for lying." I covered my mouth.

"You don't have to worry about him again." He closed the towel and towered over me.

No words were spoken as I placed my hands on the bottom of his shirt. I lifted it up and he assisted by removing it all the way. I fumbled a little with the button on his jeans, unzipped them and pulled them down along with his boxers. His body was magnificent just as I imagined. He kicked his shoes off and I finished stripping him. He stood there naked and my body reacted quickly.

"Stay right here." I ran in the kitchen and grabbed the honey. I always wanted to try this on someone and since he's here; why not.

"What's that?" I hid it behind my back.

"Lay down." He did what I asked and moved to the top of my queen size bed. His feet were hanging off but who cares. I flipped the light switch off, and turned on the light on my nightstand that I kept a purple bulb in. I grabbed my phone and turned Pandora on to Blackstreet radio and did my thing.

I let the honey drip down on his lips first and kissed and sucked it off. I moved down to his chest with it and as you know, honey pours out slow, so I enjoyed watching him squirm as it hit his skin. I covered his bellybutton, his manhood, in between his legs and down to his feet.

"Oh shit Zakiya." I circled his chest with my tongue and slid down to his belly button where some of the honey sat. I allowed my tongue to roam the rest of his body.

I was now in between, licking up and down his leg. His manhood was semi erect, and I couldn't wait to taste him. Not only was he big and thick, he was long, which meant he's about to hit every spot inside me and I'm anticipating it.

I took his dick in my mouth and began sucking to get him fully erect and let the tip rub against the roof of mouth. I sucked and bobbed my head slowly only to hear his throaty moan. I stared up at him and he was on his elbows enjoying the show. The lust gracing his face made a smile come across mine, as I lifted his dick and juggled both of his balls inside my mouth.

"Keep going Za." He moaned out giving me a nickname.

I let the tip touch the back of my throat and started humming. I saw it on a porn site, and I'll be damned if it didn't work. His breathing sped up, his toes curled, he let out another moan and released. I made it real nasty for him, and I could tell he appreciated it.

I crawled up to him and placed kisses on his chest before allowing our mouths to meet. I loved the way he kissed. It wasn't too rough or to slow. It was perfect and enough to start my juices flowing.

I could feel his fingers running up and down my bare pussy. He teased my clit a few times by touching it lightly and then dipping two fingers inside. He gently slid me onto my stomach, lifted me up a little and moved his fingers back where they were.

His dick was growing, and I felt him just inches away from my throbbing pussy. I attempted to move downward to insert him in since he was teasing me, but he'd pull back. His lips were now placing kisses on my spine. Each one made my body tingle. Before I could say anything, my legs were spread apart and he was now under me with my pussy on his face.

"Fuck Consequence. It feels so good." His tongue was buried in between my folds and flickering over my clit. A bitch was in heaven.

"Cum Zakiya." He managed to say in between licking and sucking. He slid two fingers in, and I lost it. My body exploded and he lapped up every bit of juice he could. I was ready for bed.

"Don't get tired. We not done." He flipped me over, climbed on top and grabbed a hold of my hips. My legs were now on his shoulders, which gave him a perfect view; well from what he could see being the room is dim.

"Oh fuck." My nails dug into his biceps when he first entered. All you heard was skin smacking and both of us expressing how good it felt. I couldn't move and once he pummeled back down after pulling out, he groaned deeply, letting me know he was enjoying it even more.

Consequence picked up speed and with every stroke, his balls were slapping my ass. His dick was hitting my cervix and that's when his hand went around my throat. The thrill and excitement of him doing it and staring in my eyes, made me cum hard as hell. I don't ever remember this happening.

"Damn girl. You got some good pussy." He had me turn over and kept the pace.

I grabbed the pillow and moaned into it so my neighbors wouldn't hear me, but it was no use. He was fucking me too good. The pleasurable pain had my eyes rolling and stomach tightening. I knew another orgasm was coming and so did he.

"That pussy contracting real nice."

SMACK! He smacked me and I started throwing it back.

"You like this dick Za?" He snatched the back of my hair and pulled me up.

"Yes. Oh, gawd yes." His fingers were circling my clit as my back stuck to his chest.

"You want me to keep fucking you after tonight?"

"Yes." He turned my face to him and threw his tongue in my mouth. My hand was on the back of his neck as he circled faster, making my clit harder.

"Arch that back sexy." He pushed me back on down and started moving faster. The force he used to enter was outta this world. It's like he wanted me to feel him deep and I did.

"Got dammit, this feels good. Don't stop Consequence.

I'm gonna cum." His hands gripped my hips as he pumped harder, with his dick damn near touching my chest.

"Fuck me baby. Yea just like that." I moaned.

"Like this Za?" He stopped, lifted me up and fucked me standing up. I don't know how he's able to do it and I don't care.

"Suck this nut out." I hopped off, squatted down in front of him and accepted every baby he let out.

"Fuck! That was good." He leaned against the wall for a second staring.

"What?"

"I'm no good for you Zakiya but I want you." I moved over to him and wrapped my arms around his neck. We were both sweaty and sticky.

"I'm perfect for you and I want you too, but I understand. Just know, that after tonight this won't happen again."

"Why not?" He asked.

"Feelings will eventually get involved and I don't wanna get hurt. So..." I kissed his lips and backed away with his hand in mine.

"Let's finish in the shower and if I'm not too sore, again after. But once you walk out the door that's it." He didn't say a word and followed me in the bathroom.

"This is a decent bathroom." I shook my head and started the shower.

"It's the hood, but I'm very clean."

"You better be. I just stuck my dick in you with no rubber."

"If anyone should be nervous, it's me because you are definitely having sex with others."

"You're not?" He questioned as if I'm supposed to be.

"The last time was two years ago with my ex. He cheated, I got tested twice for everything and I've been celibate ever since."

"Your landlord."

"It happened when I first moved on my own five years ago. If you wanna know has he tried; absolutely but I'm good. Those few times were just to get me through some rough patches." He nodded and turned me around.

"You don't have a fake body, plastic breasts or nothing do you?" I turned my head over my shoulder.

"Everything you touch is real baby." He smirked.

"Good because if I ever want another kid, you may be the mother."

"What?" He pulled my lower half away from the wall, bent me over and had me moaning very loud.

By the time we finished doing freaky shit to one another, it was after three in the morning. He put his clothes on and I walked him to the door. Something about him leaving felt funny. I wanted to ask him to stay the night but once he got dressed, I didn't bother.

"Keep lil Con safe." He nodded.

"Do you mind if he calls to talk to you?"

"You think he'll want to?" I asked.

"He's seen other women speak to me and has been around Lisa for a long time and not once did he ever have a connection with anyone besides you. As you can see, he wants a mother but that's not why I want you to talk to him. I think you're the closest thing to what he thinks a mother should be."

"Are you sure?" He leaned down and placed a sensual kiss on my lips.

"Positive. Take care and if you need me..." I'm cut him off.

"You've done enough, and I appreciate all of it. Get home safe." I waited for him to pull off, locked up and went straight to sleep. I had a great night.

CHAPTER 13

Andrina

"How much longer before you speak?" I jumped hearing Rage's voice. I got off work an hour ago and stopped by the grocery store. I had no idea he was here or for how long.

"What are you doing here?"

"Why wouldn't I be?" He removed the bags from my hand and brought them in the kitchen.

"Is it more?"

"Just a few but I can get them." He walked out the door and a few minutes later, returned with the rest. He placed them on the counter and followed me in the bedroom. I took my shoes off, put my slippers on and tried to go in the kitchen but he stopped me.

"Come here." He led me in the bathroom and I almost cried looking at the candies lit and rose petals in the tub.

"I'll put the food away." I nodded and let him take my uniform off first and then my panties and bra.

"Is it cold? I started it right before you pulled in."

"It's warm." He held my hand as I stepped in. I sat down and laid my head on the bath pillow. It felt good and my body began relaxing right away.

"I'll be right back." I don't know how long he was gone because I dosed off. I do know he had his sleeves rolled up when my eyes opened.

"I'm about to wash you up, give you a massage and lay next to you all night." I smiled and stood for him to wash me. He let the water out and rinsed me off with the shower.

"You don't have to do all this. Oh shit! Right there." I moaned out when he rubbed my feet. I've been working nonstop because Zakiya and I were moving in together.

The night she spent with Consequence made her realize she wanted more outta life. She always has but when you actually witness the wealth and what it can do for you, you try to escalate the process.

She mentioned almost whooping some chick's ass and how his son loved her immediately. I don't think I've ever seen her smile as much as she did speaking about anyone except Consequence. She didn't go into detail with everything and it wasn't hard to tell he strung her out. I knew she was feeling his aggressive ass from the first day in Walmart.

Somehow, they continued running into one another and each rude comment he made, made her want him more. I truly believe he gets a kick outta her reactions, which is why he bothered her as much as he did. Now that they've crossed the line, they haven't spoken or seen one another. His mom did reach out a few times a week for the little boy to talk to her. I think they're supposed to link up so he can see her.

"You deserve it." He continued and I found myself becoming aroused.

"You a'ight?" He asked because my body had a mind if its own.

"I'm ok."

"Don't look like it." He removed his shirt, shut the light off and stared down at me.

"Did I ever mention how sexy you are?"

"You did but what are you..." I didn't finish my sentence because he parted my legs and attacked my clit forcefully with his mouth.

"Courage, this is not... oh gawd... don't stop." I bunched the sheets up in my hand and came extremely hard. He didn't stop until I cried out. All I wanted to do is sleep but it's been a month since we've seen one another. I knew he wasn't leaving.

"Get on top." He made himself comfortable on the bed and his back sat against the headboard. He placed his hands on my hips as I stood over him and he stared at my juices glistened down my legs. I moved down slowly and the second his tip touched my pussy, he thrusted inside before I could object.

"Fuck, I missed this Drina." He guided me slowly in circles; moaning each time.

"Sorry ma." He laughed when his dick went limp and slid

outta me. He said he hasn't been with anyone since the last time we were together. Its why he came so fast.

"Rage, I don't want any kids." He snatched my hair and forced his tongue in. The kissing turned aggressive and his manhood began to grow again. When he was fully erect, my hands went to his chest. Each time I moved down his shaft, he'd thrust harder. He buried himself as deep as he could in this position making sure I felt every inch of him.

"Fuck me harder Courage. Make me regret breaking up with you." He flipped me on my back and positioned himself perfectly. He loved watching my facial expressions as he took me to ecstasy.

"Don't stop baby. Oh gawd, I missed this dick." I screamed out with my hand over my head trying to match his thrusts. It felt like my pussy walls were about to come down by how hard he was going.

"You like me fucking you hard Drina?" I nodded and bit down on my lip.

"You're gonna have my kid." His kissed me hard again and slowed down.

"I love you Andrina and one day, you're gonna be my wife." I don't know why his words brought tears to my eyes, but they did.

"I've never cheated on you and I won't. I miss you ma." My hands went to the side of his face.

"You better not make me a single mother." He smiled and made love to me for the rest of the night.

"You'll never be a single mother because I'm not leaving

you. As far as money, you set for life baby." My head was on his chest after we finished.

"I don't want your money unless it's for the baby and even then, you can buy the stuff." He turned my face to him.

"I'm gonna set you up with a bank account."

"No Courage." He shushed me with his finger and told me to go to sleep. He better not give me money. I refuse to have his family thinking I got pregnant on purpose or that I need him.

I laughed to myself; why did I let this nigga get me pregnant? I took one last look at him and closed my eyes. I hope I made the right choice.

* * *

"Bitch, you let that nigga bust inside you?" Zakiya said as we moved the totes into another room.

She was helping me get the stuff ready for the movers. It's been a week since I've seen Courage because he went outta town and I hadn't told him about the move. He'd just try and make me stay with him and I didn't want that. I mean, I could but I would be putting Zakiya in a bad position. She was tired of the hood and I didn't blame her.

"He was fucking me so good Zakiya. Shit, I was lost in the moment."

"Consequence fucked me good too, but I made sure he pulled out. I even went to the doctor to get tested the next day. Girl, you crazy." She shook her head.

"Courage and I been together longer, and I agree, it's early and he has a kid on the way. I should've thought it through, and I didn't. I tried to grab a Plan b from Walgreens, and do you know, this big black guard looking guy walked up and said, *I wouldn't do that if I were you.*"

"What? Bitch, he having you followed?"

"I think Courage knew it was the heat of the moment for me." We both laughed.

"Did you know him and Consequence we're brothers?" She asked confusing me.

"Brothers? No, I was supposed to meet his family a while back but then I broke up with him. That's crazy. Consequence and Courage? What were their parents thinking?" I looked at her.

"What?"

"Why is their sister named Conscience?"

"I know you lying."

"Nope."

"Wait! What are the parents name?" I asked.

"Who knows? I called them by their last names. Ain't it crazy tho?"

"Ugh, yea."

KNOCK! KNOCK! The door was cracked for the movers so neither of us moved.

"Who the fuck are you?" I barked.

"Why are you here Ciara?" Zakiya asked.

"Ciara as in the bitch who tagged me on Instagram?" She

tagged me on the photo, but I couldn't see her photos since she was private.

"Oh, y'all friends?" She questioned Zakiya as if they were affiliated.

"Best friends. Again, why are you here?"

"No beef with you Zakiya but I do have an issue with this ho sleeping with my man."

"Ho? You got me confused. As far as Courage being your man, I'm confused becasue to my knowledge, he and I are together and you're just his baby momma for the time being." I could see her getting upset. I picked my phone up and called him. I'm not about to play these games with her.

"Hey babe. What's up?"

"Babe, I have you on speaker because Ciara stopped by saying I'm sleeping with her man. I'm confused because we're together. Can you clear this up?"

"Ciara stop playing yourself. I haven't fucked you since the night you got pregnant. You haven't sucked my dick and nothing sexual has happened between us. You were at the house for dinner because my mom invited you and I left you right there when it was over. I'm not gonna tell you again to stay away from my girl. The next time, I'm just gonna show you and if you lose the baby in the process so be it."

"Babe, don't say that." Ciara had tears streaming down her face.

"Nah. I'm not about to let her fuck up shit between us. Beat it bitch. Matter of fact, wait right there. I'll call you back Drina." He hung up and we stared at her.

"You need help leaving?" Zakiya asked.

"Fuck you bitch and Zakiya, I hope you don't think fucking Consequence means he left Lisa alone. They're still fucking and if he made you his woman too, he's gonna cheat on you with Lisa, just like he did with his wife."

"Wife?" Zakiya snapped.

"Like I said, Lisa is his ride or die and I am the same for Rage."

"Rage?" I was confused.

"It's his street name but I guess your bougie ass wouldn't know that." Ciara snapped.

"You can go now." I waved her off.

"Don't get comfortable because we all know when this baby comes, you'll be pushed to the side."

"Let's go." That same guard stood in the hallway.

"Tell him, I'll be at the house waiting for him to drop me off food or whatever else I ask for." She smirked.

"That billionaire dick good Andrina and I ain't giving it up. Why you think I got pregnant on purpose?" She said low and we heard her.

"Billionaire?"

"You stupid as fuck. Peace." The guard pushed her down the hall and I looked at Zakiya who was as confused as me.

"What is she talking about billionaire?"

"Girl, I don't know. Maybe she talking about it's worth billions." She shrugged and we finished bringing everything to the living room.

"When are you gonna tell him about the move?" Zakiya asked when we sat in the car. The movers were pulling off.

"He's gone for two more weeks. If he wants me, I'm sure he can find me." I said and drove in front of her. Goodbye old place, hello new.

CHAPTER 14

Lisa

"Shit baby. Yes, it feels good. Don't stop." I bit down on the pillow as Consequence plowed into me from behind.

"Right there. Oh shit." I released and felt him pull out before releasing himself. He's never cum inside me even with the condom on.

In the beginning, I was offended but now, I could care less. Let me explain my position in this man's life so people can get a better understanding of what we share.

"I'm Lisa Hopkins and Consequence and I, have the normal girl meets boy story. We grew up as neighbors in a rich area and became close; very close. He was my first and I was his. It didn't make either of us fall in love because we had no idea what we were doing.

We were both fourteen at the time and exploring one another. He had a little girlfriend because even as a young teenager, Consequence was fine. The little bitches would go crazy over him and yet, I'm the only one at the time he was sleeping with.

Anytime we wanted to try a new sexual position, we'd call on each other. We were each other's guinea pigs until the age of sixteen, when he really matured. His body was amazing and by this time, we were fucking like porn stars.

To this very day, he has never claimed me as his woman no matter how connected we are. Our sexual chemistry is outta this world and regardless who he's with, I'm always going to be the one he comes back to. Shit, he married Lauren, and I still sucked him off when necessary. Its not my fault he's finding women who can't satisfy him.

This bitch Zakiya is gonna be a problem though; especially since his son seems to be smitten by her. Don't get me wrong, she's a pretty woman but what can he possibly see in a hood chick?

I'm sure she can cook, smoke weed and do hair but intellectually, what can she do? Can she uplift his mind or channel his aggressive behavior the way I do? No woman will stick around for half the shit Consequence does.

He's always been rude, and arrogant but again, as he grew older and learned more, his demeanor is worse. I think the day he caught Lauren cheating; it broke him. He believed she was the woman he belonged with. The woman to bear all his kids and grow old with. I admit, I was shocked myself when Conscience told me.

Yea, I was happy the marriage was over because it meant

more quality time for me. However; no one saw him for a couple months. His parents and siblings spoke to him but outside of them, it's like he disappeared. Not one peep.

It wasn't until his mom threw lil Con a party at her house. He showed up and guess who went to a hotel with him. Yup! I sure did and we've been back at it ever since.

"You staying over?" I asked when he walked out the bathroom.

He never left the condom in the trash and watched it go down the toilet. I'm desperate for his love and attention but not enough to steal his sperm. He'd kill me and I'm not tryna die. If he wants me to have a child with him, then I will.

"Nah, I got some things to take care of and ma taking Lil Con to see Zakiya." I sat up with my knees to my chest.

"You're ok with that?" He looked up as he slid his foot in his sneaker.

"Why wouldn't I be?"

"I don't know. Maybe because y'all aren't a couple and it may give him false hope on ever having a mother figure in his life." He chuckled.

"It's not giving him false hope because he knows Zakiya and I aren't a couple. He's spoken to her on the phone through my mom plenty of times and even Face Timed her." He stood and grabbed his keys.

"The day she saved him at the store, he connected with her. Now whether it be in a motherly way or not, I don't care. He adores her and she feels the same. Why would I snatch that away from him?"

"I'm not saying do that. It's just weird to see another woman around that's not his mom." He smirked and moved towards me.

"You've been in his life since before he entered this world. You watched him grow even when his mother left. How many times did you step in and say, Consequence I'll take him to the park? Or how many times did you call or come over to my parents to check on him without looking for me? Did you ever try and be a mother figure with him? Not that you had to but now all of a sudden you're concerned because it's with someone you don't know."

"You don't know her either."

"You're right but I know a lot more than you think. You must be a fool to assume I'd let my son out with anyone unattended." He lifted my face.

"You were my first sexual experience, my side chick, then my mistress. Now you're back to just being the woman I fuck. Do I need to change that?" I didn't say anything.

"I can't hear you."

"No."

"Don't worry about who my son is around. He's my concern; not yours."

"Whatever." He left out the room and I heard the door close. Why do I even bother?

"What up Lisa?" Rock said opening the door. Conscience and I were going shopping with her mom.

"Hey." He closed the door behind me and walked in the other room.

"I'll be right down Lisa." Conscience yelled from the top of the stairs.

"I'm going to run to the bathroom." I went to use the one in the back and overheard Rock talking.

"Zakiya Summers. I need her found and brought to me." I stood and listened without making a sound. I couldn't hear the person on the other line responding but I damn sure heard him.

"Yea. It's been a long time since I've seen her. I miss the hell outta her." My mouth hit the floor.

"I'm ready Lisa." I never even used the bathroom.

"You out babe?" Rock came from the back and kissed her neck.

"Yea."

"Hurry up back. I got something for you." She smiled and it pissed me off. How he looking for another bitch and rubbing all up on her? Men ain't shit.

"See you later." I stepped out when they started kissing.

"You ok?" Conscience asked on the way to the car.

"Yea. Just got a lot on my mind." We sat down in the car and closed the door.

"Look Lisa. I understand you and my brother been around each other for years and he has you living comfortably. If you wanna keep the lifestyles he's affording you, it's best you keep your comments to yourself and if he does get in a relationship with someone, keep quiet. Otherwise; he's going to take it all away." I stayed quiet.

"Bad enough, I was caught in the middle of y'all shit."

"Really Conscience?" She looked at me.

"Hell yea really. I don't play that side chick or mistress shit. I've been cheated on, so I know what it's like to feel less of a woman over it." If she only knew. I kept my thoughts to myself.

During the course of her brother's relationship with Lauren, he used going to her house a lot as an excuse to slip out and be with me. Eventually, Lauren caught on and it caused them to stop speaking. Conscience didn't care because at the end of the day, Consequence is her brother. She's gonna always have his back.

"All I'm saying is, stop waiting around for Consequence. You're a good woman, who has a decent job and can have any man she wants. No need to sit back hoping and praying my brother will pick you because we both know he's not. All you are to him is a fuck." I sucked my teeth.

"I don't wanna discuss him anymore."

"Ok then. What you buying?" My mind was in overdrive from what she said, what I heard from her man and what's going on between Consequence and me. I should drop her off to her mother and keep it moving. Then again, maybe shopping will help.

CHAPTER 15
Zakiya

"Hey sweetie. How are you?" I hugged Lil Con tight. I've been seeing him as much as I could since he's asked.

The first time, I was pretty nervous because I don't want to portray his mother but it's hard when he wants one so bad. Mrs. Waters said, he sees the kids at school with their mom and he wants the same. It's understandable but I still don't want him confused.

"Hey." I was shocked to see his father bringing him to the mall. Mrs. Waters is usually the mediator. I admit he was looking good as hell tho.

"Hey. How you been?" I took the small bag from him. Lil Con asked if he could stay the night and his father told him yes. Another surprise from me but I could tell Consequence gave him whatever he wanted as long as it made sense.

"I'm good. You?"

"Working a lot. We just moved..." I told him.

"We?" I chuckled at the slight jealousy.

"Me and Andrina rented a three bedroom. Now that I'm making extra money from this rude guy I met, which I still don't know how you made it happen. But anyway, we decided to put our money together and get something better in a different neighborhood. I'm sure you know that." I opened my car door.

"I do but you could've told me." I leaned in the car to put Lil Con's seatbelt on and felt him pressing against my ass. I backed up and closed the door.

"We..." I pointed between the two of us.

"We agreed you weren't good for me and I understood. Remember? This will never happen." I pointed between us again.

"You're right but yo, on the real, I've never had any woman do the things you did to me and I've had a lot." I rolled my eyes.

"Well whoever you sleeping with, tell her to do it. Let her know you wanna be freaky."

"For some reason, I only want you to do it." I swallowed hard and stared up at him. I needed to divert my eyes quickly because he has the ability to make me say yes with that smile and those eyes.

"Not sure what affect you have on me but it's something." He said kissing the side of my neck.

"I'm not going to bother you." He stopped and looked in the car. Lil Con was playing with his phone. Consequence lifted my head to make me look at him.

"Take care of my son." He pressed his lips on mine and I couldn't help it. I wrapped my arms around his neck and my legs went around his waist.

"You want this dick, don't you?"

"You messed the whole mood up." I pushed him gently to open my door.

"It's not like we can fuck out here. Well, we could by my son here."

"Bye Consequence."

"Have him call me later. Oh, and he's allergic to..."

"Strawberries and bananas. I know Consequence. Your mom reminds me everytime." He smiled and opened the back door.

"A'ight son. Call me before you go to bed." He hugged him and kissed his forehead. I loved the bond he had with Lil Con.

At first, I thought he was never home but it's not the case. He's always there and if his son stays at his parents, then he does as well so they can wake up together.

"Bye." He closed the door and I pulled off. I saw him shaking his head in the rear-view mirror.

********************************.

"Ok bitch. It's about time we get to celebrate your promotion." Andrina said drinking her Martini. We were at one of the hottest clubs in Miami and it was packed.

"Whatever. We had a lot going on." I said.

"Yea ok."

"Anyway. What's up with you? You're barely at the house and when you are, so is Courage."

"Girl, he not letting me outta his sight. Talking about he wants to see me everyday with his baby in my stomach."

"Did you take a test yet?"

"No. I think I am though because it's been a month and a half and there's no sight of my period. Ever since the first time he let his babies off inside, he hasn't stopped."

"Nasty. Have you met his parents yet?"

"Is it crazy to say I haven't?" I gave her a crazy look.

"I asked why he never invited me, and he claims it's because its complicated. He mentioned me to them before but then I broke up with him. They think he's single. Do you think he's cheating?" Her eyes were becoming glassy.

"He better not be. You know we jump niggas."

"We ain't jumping him tho." She laughed and used her forefingers to catch the tears before they fell.

"Hell no. Him or his crazy ass brother. I bet the sister just as violent." I took a sip of my drink.

"Yup. I think he may be messing with the baby mama." I sat my drink on the table.

We weren't in a VIP area, but we were sitting at one of the small tables on the side of the dance floor. There were a bunch of them and if you didn't have one, you were stuck standing. I can't tell you how many females in here holding their heels.

"I don't think so. He literally bombed her on the phone with you."

"I know but what if it was fake?" She was thinking too much.

"Fake?"

"You mean planned?" I asked to make sure we were speaking on the same thing.

"What if he said to her, *if you ever see my girl you better not tell. What if...*" I stopped her.

"Andrina, you're thinking too much into it. Now I don't agree with him not introducing you because I've met them, and this is before I slept with the brother. I do feel you need to talk to him and see what's up. You're with him all the time. It doesn't make any sense."

"It doesn't and that's the only reason I can come up with. Maybe he still brings her to the house like they're one big happy family."

"The day I was there, Consequence told Ciara in her face they're not sure if the baby is his brothers. Maybe he's tryna keep the peace for now. Who knows?" I took another sip and almost choked when he walked in.

"Damn bitch. He looks good as hell right now but why is he with her?" I poured myself a cup of Cîroc and drank it straight. We had to order bottle service because the waitresses were taking forever just to bring one drink.

"I don't know and I don't care." I pretended not to care.

"If you don't, then why are you getting upset?"

"Fuck him Andrina."

"You did and that's why you're mad. Zakiya, you told him no sex so where you think he's gonna get it from?"

"Not that bitch." I poured another cup of Cîroc and this time, I filled it with some pineapple juice. Drinking it straight is too much.

"Why is Rage here?" She stood and I sat her down.

"I thought he wasn't returning until tomorrow."

"He may have just got in. Don't flip out sis. I don't even want them to know we're here."

"Why?"

"I wanna see how he treats the Lisa bitch when I'm not around." I said watching them walk to the third floor. You could tell it was exclusive just by the amount of security it held.

"Ain't no woman gonna stick around a nigga who constantly treats them like shit." She said and I would agree had it been someone else.

"She would because she's desperate."

"Well we can't see from down here." I kept my eyes on Consequence at the top of the club. In a sense, I wanted him to see me and in another, I wanted to peep how he treated her. Why is she even up there if he don't fuck with her like that?

"You ok?"

"I should be asking you that." I pointed to Rage who had a woman standing in front of him. His head was down on the phone and seconds later, Andrina phone lit up.

"Look at this."

Hey. I got back early and stopped by the club with my brother. I'll be there when we leave. Love you.

"Well at least he's honest."

"I guess." She responded and put the phone down.

"You wanna dance?" She asked.

"Yup."

"Either stay in your seat or you gotta go." Someone said the second our feet hit the floor.

"Excuse me." I gave him a dirty look.

"Boss said, nothing gets passed him." He shrugged and I looked up. Consequence stood in front of the banister with his back turned and his arms on the rails. He wasn't even looking down here; yet, had someone watching me.

"Tell boss... You know what? Never mind. We going up there." He moved out the way and another guard escorted us to the third floor. Security lifted the rope and the two of us walked through.

The place was amazing. There was another dance floor with a live DJ and you can't tell but it's a glass surrounding the area and you couldn't hear the music from the other floors. Couches were lined up and you could tell only people with money graced this floor.

"Why you here?" Rage barked and snatched up Andrina.

"Nice place." I stood next to Consequence who had his eyes on someone.

"Why you in here dressed like these ho's?" He pulled me in front of him.

"Why does it matter? You're here with someone else and

you never know. I may take someone..." He wrapped his hand around my hair and tilted my head back.

"You going home with who?" He gripped it tighter.

"Let go Consequence." I tried to pry his hands off.

"Nah. You wanna play games right."

"You're not my man."

"You right." He let go and pushed me away from him.

"Come here Lisa." She didn't see me at first but when she did, her face turned up.

"You got that pussy ready for tonight?"

"Always."

"Good. Somebody pissed me off so I'm taking it out on you."

"I wouldn't have it any other way." She kissed his cheek and slid her hand up his chest.

"A'ight. She get it. You doing too much." He pushed her away and turned to me.

"Why the fuck you still up here? You wanna go home with a nigga, right? Bounce."

"You are so got damn aggressive and ignorant." I shouted.

"You know this and still come around."

"Not anymore." I went to walk off and he grabbed me by the back of my neck.

"Do what the fuck you want. I don't care, but if my son calls or wants to come see you, you better make it happen. Are we clear?" I had tears running down my face.

"I would never do that to him Consequence. Let me go." My hands were trying to move his.

"Tough hood bitches don't cry. Fix your face and straighten the fuck up." Is he serious? He damn near choking me and telling me to stop crying.

"You're better than her. Everything about you makes her jealous. Get it together Zakiya. Don't ever let her see you as a weak bitch." He pushed me away and told me I better not turn around for her to see me crying.

"Rage will take your friend home. Good night." He shouted and I never turned around. He's right. Lisa was probably watching, and I wouldn't give her the satisfaction.

I stormed out the club and for a second, I swore Rock was getting out of a car with some chick. I hadn't seen him in years. I felt a presence behind me, and it was that big ass bodyguard who threw me on the ground at Walmart.

"What?"

"Boss wants me to make sure you get home."

"Fuck your boss. Tell him to stay the fuck away from me." He chuckled.

"Right now. He's doing what's best for you, even though you don't know it."

"Whatever." I got to my car and Andrina was being walked out by a guard herself.

"What you doing here? I thought Rage was taking you home."

"He said his pregnant woman has no business in a club without him." We sat down in the car and pulled off. *Fuck Consequence.*

CHAPTER 16
Consequence

"She so damn hardheaded." Rage stood next to me speaking of his girl.

"Why they here?"

"Celebrating the promotion you gave Zakiya. It's the first time they've been out." I nodded.

"Everyone in place?"

"Yup." He leaned against the rail with me as we watched our prey who had no idea what was going on.

"Why Lisa here?"

"The bitch was here before me and once security saw her, they let her come in. I tried to ditch her knowing Zakiya was here but she's like a damn leech." Rage arrived a few minutes after me because he just came in from outta town. Lisa was in line and saw me pull up.

I had already received the call Zakiya was here and didn't want no shit. I knew Lisa would be smart and tonight wasn't the time. I had her come to the third floor to stay away from Zakiya but they saw one another anyway. No one knew about Andrina yet, which is why Rage didn't know she was inside.

"That's yo fault. Ma dukes told you to let her go."

"I will. Soon as Zakiya and I are on the same page." He busted out laughing.

"Bro, she ain't fucking with you." I turned my head.

"Why you say that?"

"You too damn mean for her from what Drina says. One minute you're nice and the next you turn into someone else. She called you Dr. Jekyll and Mr. Hyde." I shook my head.

"I'm tryna feel her out and at the same time see if she's right for Lil Con."

"She has him a lot bro. If she wasn't wifey or mother material, you wouldn't even let him go, so stop denying what you feeling for her."

"And that's what expert?"

"You like her more than you want. She gives you a run for your money and fucked you real well; better than anyone you've been with. Shit, you won't let her be with anyone else so do what you gotta do before she really stops fucking with you. What you waiting for?" I thought about what he said and he's right. A woman will only tolerate so much, and she's dealt with a lot from me thus far.

"There he is. You ready?" Rage said and we put our game face on.

"You already know." I walked over to where the dude Carlos was, that I've been searching for.

Carlos wasn't rich but somehow, he came into some money. In order to step in this section, you had to prove you had some. I'm guessing the bag next to him with bills hanging out did the trick.

He's the guy who almost kidnapped my son. For a minute, I thought it was one of the guards and come to find out, it wasn't. It eased my mind and I think it did for Ron too. He knew how I felt about weak niggas and disloyalty.

"Carlos my man." He had two women on him as others sat in his area tryna fuck. I don't really care what people do here, as long as it doesn't stop my money, we good.

"Who the fuck are you?"

"Is that anyway to speak to the man whose son you tried to kidnap?" His facial expression changed.

"Get the fuck on." I told the bitches on his lap.

"We don't have to go anywhere."

"Oh no." Rage laid both of them out. Bullets straight to their forehead.

"Don't nobody fucking move." I said and kept my gun trained on Carlos.

"Take him out." He shouted and five guys stood with weapons.

"You insult me Carlos." I nodded and Ron, John, two other guys, two of my waitresses, the bartender and the DJ, all pulled their weapons out. I always make sure my people strapped just in case.

"Consequence what's going on?" I could've smacked the fuck out Lisa for opening her mouth. She had no idea what was going on and because she wanted to be clingy, she caught up. She better hope she doesn't die.

"Ron take this piece of shit out back." He snatched Carlos up and one guy took a shot catching me in the arm. He didn't have a silencer and all hell broke loose. You could see the lights flashing from up here and people must've known because they were running, and bodies were dropping.

"GET MY BROTHER OUTTA HERE!" Rage shouted and John walked me down the stairs.

"I'm good. Get Rage before he kills everyone in there over me." He opened the door for me to get in and closed it to run back in. A few minutes later, he ran out with Rage and the other guys.

"Let me get you to a hospital." He jumped on the driver's side and sped off. At least, we got the motherfucker.

* * *

"What Consequence?" She hadn't turned over or even heard me come through the door because her friend opened it. I tried to move around and almost fell because it was dark as hell in here.

I had a key here too, but she didn't know. I'll never just walk in if Andrina here tho. I thought about stopping by last night but after surgery, I went to my parents. I refused to lay up in a hospital.

"I wanted to make sure you were good."

"I'm fine. Tough, hood bitches don't cry right. You can go now." I sat on the bed struggling to take my shoes off.

"Can you help me?" I had a sling on. The bullet went through my shoulder and exited out the back. It was a clean shot.

"Help you what? I told your aggressive ass to leave." She reached over and turned the small light from her nightstand on.

"What happened to you? Are you ok?"

"I got shot last night."

"Oh my God." She kneeled down to untie my sneakers. I lifted her head.

"It's the reason I made you leave."

"You knew you were gonna get shot? I'm confused." She pulled both of my sneakers off and had me stand to take my jeans off as well.

"I knew it was a possibility, which is why I had you go. I didn't wanna take the chance of you getting hurt." She helped me get comfortable in the bed. I had to laugh a little because she told me to leave and yet, helping me stay.

"Not like you care." She went to walk away, and I grabbed her wrist.

"I do care Zakiya. I care too much that's why it's fucking with me. I'm not supposed to want you the way I do. Hell, sometimes I find myself needing you and I don't know why."

"I want and need you too, but you said it yourself, you're no good for me. I'm not trying to get hurt and you and her are sleeping together. I'm not ok with that, nor will I ever be."

"Can you get me some water and reach in my pocket to grab the pain pill?" I ignored the last part. She walked out and came back with the water and grabbed the pill. I took it and had her sit next to me.

"I'm fucking her for sure it's not a secret." She sucked her teeth.

"We're not together Zakiya but I swear, if we were, I wouldn't dare stick my dick in her."

"Are you married?" I stiffened up when she asked.

"Oh my God! I'm sleeping with a married man. I'm really a ho." She started pacing back and forth making me dizzy.

"ZAKIYA!" She stopped.

"Sit." I patted the seat next to me.

"No. You're married and..."

"SIT GOT DAMMIT!" She jumped and did like I asked. I rested my head on the pillow.

"Ten years ago, I met a woman named Lauren. She was beautiful, and smart. We fell in love, had a son, and were living happily ever after or so I thought. I did any and everything for her; including giving her an endless bank account and having a house built from the ground up. It was nothing I wouldn't do for her."

"If it's making you upset, we don't have to talk about it." She intertwined her hands in mine and it made me calmer. What is she doing to me?

"It's ok. Anyway, I came home from work one day and caught her by surprise or should I say, she caught me."

"What you mean?"

"She had on a robe with tassels hanging off her breasts and looked like she had just been fucked."

"Not in y'all house."

"Exactly. Long story short, I go in the room and some nigga had a gun pointing in my face." She covered her mouth.

"I beat him until he was unrecognizable, drug him down the stairs and out the back door. I burned him alive, along with the house and car I brought her. I drove her to the clinic, had my peoples give her an abortion, told the bitch not to ever contact me again and ran her dumb ass over as I pulled out."

"Wow."

"I thought I hated the bitch then but nah. I hate her even more now because yea, I told her not to contact me, but we have a son. A son who's so desperate for a mother's love, he latched on to you. No offense."

"None taken. I get it."

"Do you because I really want my son to know what's it like to have a mother's love."

"I know you do."

"I'm not pushing him on you by no means but on some real shit Zakiya, he loves you."

"I love him too." I smiled when she said it.

"How long has his mother been gone?"

"The bitch ain't his mother and this happened when he was barely one. I haven't seen or heard from the bitch since."

"That's crazy. I could never leave my child no matter how bad my situation is." I wrapped my hand around the back of her neck and pulled her close.

"Rage says, I need to tell you how I really feel." It felt like I was stuttering.

"The pills must be kicking in. Go to sleep babe."

"Babe? I'm your babe Zakiya?" She started laughing.

"You are very mean and aggressive, but you are my babe." I felt her lips on mine and stuck my tongue inside her mouth.

"Another time Consequence. The meds are kicking in and we don't have any condoms." She pulled away and had me lay flat.

"Good night." She kissed me again, laid in front of me and put my arm across her stomach.

"Night." She moved my hand to her mouth and kissed it. I couldn't say anything because my eyes were losing the battle of staying open. I let sleep overtake me.

CHAPTER 17
Courage

"Why the hell is my pregnant girlfriend at the club?" I dropped my brother off at their crib and brought Andrina to mine. Zakiya can talk shit all she wants but she ain't going nowhere.

I didn't see Drina the night before because I stayed at the hospital and then my parents' house with Consequence. I blew the niggas head off that shot him.

Anyway, my parents were mad he was hit, and I think angrier that Andrina and Zakiya were there. They knew about my girl and wanted to meet her; however, every time my mom asked me to bring her by, Ciara popped up.

She'd be on petty shit and I refused to let Andrina get caught up. I'm not ashamed of my girl whatsoever but I'm definitely not putting her in an unnecessary position either. What if she loses the baby?

I knew she was pregnant because her pussy feels different

and she hasn't gotten her period. Men are aware when their woman body changes whether they think we know it or not.

"We're not sure if I'm pregnant Courage." I took her hand in mine.

"We about to find out." I opened the bag and handed her three tests.

"Three."

"Just in case, one says positive and the other says negative. The third one can break the tie." She laughed. I was dead serious. It has to be three negatives for me to believe she's not.

"Can I go alone?"

"Why? I want us to find out together." She shook her head laughing and sat the tests on the counter. As she opened each one, my phone went off with a message from Consequence. I opened it and busted out laughing.

Tell that dirty bitch, this me all day. Don't come looking for my man. " It was a picture of my brother sleep next to Zakiya.

I received another one from Lisa asking where Consequence is because he's not at my parents. I responded with he's fine and put my phone down. I'm not getting in his shit. He'll tell her when he's ready.

"What's wrong?" Andrina had tears running down her face as she washed her hands.

"Are you cheating on me? Why can't I meet your parents? You sleeping with your ex?" As she bombarded me with questions the results of all three tests popped up.

"No, I'm not cheating on you or sleeping with Ciara. And

my parents do wanna meet the mother of my child." She looked down at the test quickly.

"Courage, are you sure you're ready? Two kids are a lot."

"I'm ready for one kid with you." I tossed two of the tests in the trash and kept one for the baby book she spoke about getting it she were expecting.

"The other chick is pregnant and..." I carried her out the bathroom.

"And until the baby is born, I don't know if it's mine." I laid her down.

"Damn, I'm happy you're having my kid." I took my shoes off and laid in bed next to her.

"You need anything?" I asked rubbing her stomach. She turned over so we were face to face.

"I need you to always protect me and this baby no matter what." Her hand went down the side of my face.

"Always."

"Good. Now tell the bitch Ciara, if she sends anything to my phone, I'm gonna whoop her ass." I used my two fingers to close her mouth.

"You ain't doing shit with my son or daughter baking inside you." She sat up, moved her legs off the bed and stood.

"You're right. Sex is off the menu too, until I deliver. It could mess up..." I hopped off the bed.

"That's never off the menu." I stripped and led her in the bathroom. She loved being in my jacuzzi, or should I say our jacuzzi? Soon she'll be Mrs. Waters so I may as well get used to saying it now.

* * *

"Where is he?" I asked Zakiya when I brought Andrina home.

"He was sleep when I walked out. I'm running late for work." She was rushing to pick her things up.

"I wonder why."

"Not for that nasty. He needs to rest. I'm late because my alarm didn't go off. Drina, I'll call you later."

"Real funny with the message." I said following her outside. I wanted to ask her a few questions about Andrina's family. If I'm gonna marry her, it's time I meet them too.

"I meant that shit." She tossed her things on the front seat.

"He told me about Lauren." I gave her a strange look.

"What?"

"He told you and you're not in the hospital or hurt?"

"Why would you ask that?"

"Because anytime he discusses her, he goes into a rage. I mean really bad."

"I could tell he was upset but he didn't raise his voice or anything like that. Look." She blew her breath in the air.

"I didn't think; no let me rephrase that. I had no plans whatsoever on messing with your brother. He's been horrible to me ever since we first laid eyes on each other. Yet; I can't help but to feel he and I are supposed to be together." I chuckled.

"I'm ok with that; however, the Lisa chick is gonna be a problem. Do you know the bitch called twenty times, sent forty text messages and a few voicemails? I had to turn the phone off after I sent you the message. The bitch asked if I were a stalker and it's clear she is."

"She is. They've been around each other since they were 14." I told her.

"Hmph." She mumbled.

"What?"

"It's why she feels entitled to be around him. I get it." She sat in her car.

"Let me get to work. Can you let him know, I'll talk to him later?" I nodded and walked back in the house.

"Your brother is awake." Drina said and pointed to the other bedroom. Consequence was yelling about something.

"Is it ok if I go in?" I asked. I'm not about to enter another woman's bedroom without permission whether she's there or not.

"Go head babe." I pushed the door open and Consequence sat on the bed looking aggravated as hell. I glanced around the room and it was decent. The whole house was actually.

"This bitch called me to..." I cut him off.

"I know. Too many times to count."

"How you know?"

"Zakiya said she had to shut the phone off because she wouldn't stop." He smiled when I mentioned her name.

"Give me a few and we can go." I turned to leave and heard him saying something.

"What you say?"

"She left me out a towel, and a toothbrush."

"Ugh. She probably thought you were gonna shower here."

"I would if I had clothes. I'll be right out." I went in the other room and Drina was in her room on the phone.

"He's fine Zakiya. Courage in there talking to him." She rolled her eyes.

"His brother taking him home." I couldn't hear what she was saying but my girl wasn't beat.

"Ok Zakiya. I'll tell him you love him."

"WHAT?" She screamed through the phone.

"Shit, that's how you're acting, asking me all these damn questions." She tossed the phone on the bed laughing.

"She hung up on me." I moved closer to her.

"I'm taking him home to change and we're gonna check on some of the businesses. You need anything while I'm out?"

"No. I'm gonna go visit my mom today. It's been a few weeks since I've seen her."

"You need me to come?" She pushed me on the bed and sat on my lap.

"No but I do want you to meet her. She's gonna love you." She kissed my neck.

"And your pops?"

"I'm not sure. He's picky with the people he likes."

"I'm picky too but I love yo sexy ass." I put my hand in her sweats and squeezed it.

"Mmm."

"Bro, if I ain't fucking, neither are you." Consequence said walking past the door.

"Looks like he's ready." She shrugged.

"Andrina, tell Zakiya I'll be by later." He shouted.

"Umm. Ok. You can call her; you know."

"Why would I do that when you can tell her?" He barked. I shook my head.

"I guess he's back to normal." She said laughing.

"See you later Courage. Be safe babe." She kissed me and got up.

"Always."

"Bye Consequence."

"Whatever." Both of us laughed. I had her lock the door and left to handle this other bullshit. I told her we were dealing with work and we will, just not right now.

CHAPTER 18

Andrina

"Bitch, you do not need to be going over there alone." Zakiya said in the phone. She was on her lunch break and I'm on my way to my parents.

"Zakiya."

"Sis, I know they're your parents and they love you. But your father blames you for what happened at his job and your mom takes his side. Andrina, it's not a good idea and if I had Courage's number, I'd tell him to go get you." I loved Zakiya as if she were my own sister.

I remember when I first started working with her, she and I clicked right away. It's weird because she's from the hood and I'm not. We live close to it now because my father kicked me out.

My mom was devastated but at least she gave me money to put down for a security deposit. She let me use her credit cards for furniture and I only purchased a cheap bedroom set, a futon for my living room and a small kitchen table. I did buy my bath-room essentials, one pot, pan, mixing bowl and some silverware for my kitchen. She was nice enough to let me use her card and I didn't want my father yelling at her because she helped me.

I had three thousand dollars in my bank account due to working but once he tossed me out, I had to literally use only what was needed. The rent was $1000 for a one bedroom and I still had utilities. It took everything in me to work at a hotel because I felt with two college degrees, it was beneath me.

Low and behold, working there I made friends, gained a sister and ended up appreciating everything more.

I'm not gonna lie, I wasn't stuck up per say but I didn't have a problem looking down on others. I had top notch every-thing at one point, thanks to my father. Gucci, Prada, Louis V; you name it, I had it. Then one man made up a lie, and it was snatched away in the blink of an eye.

That's another reason why I don't want Courage doing anything for me. What if he gets mad and takes it away and then I'm stuck with nothing? I'll be homeless with a baby. No thanks.

Zakiya and I have a three bedroom now and she already said, if I'm pregnant, which I just confirmed this morning, that the baby would get the third room.

Courage and I can co-parent because living together knowing he possibly has another child on the way, isn't gonna work. I'll be damned if that bitch comes to my house disre-specting me.

"I'm gonna be fine Zakiya. I'm pulling up now. I'll call you when I leave."

"Andrina don't mention the pregnancy unless Courage is with you."

"Ok Zakiya. I'll call you back." I turned the car off, kept my phone in my pocket and walked to the door. Here goes nothing.

*************************************.

"Hey honey. Where you been?" My mom asked. She opened the screen door for me to enter.

"Working." I stepped into the kitchen and noticed she was cooking.

"Why haven't you been around?" I gave her a strange look.

"He's getting better honey. You know you're partly to blame for the situation at work too."

"Excuse me."

"Well, they said you tried to grab the man by his balls and..."

"Ma, let me stop you right there. First of all, you know that's not true because it's not even my character to act like that." Now it was her turn to give me a crazy look.

"I may have been spoiled and turned my nose up at others,

but I never been disrespectful with it. Nor did I ever approach anyone over nonsense; especially men."

"I said the same thing until they..." I cut her off again.

"Ma, the man in question has been arrested various times and fired from other jobs due to sexual harassment. And yes, I know this because my new man searched him up." Courage looked the guy up and he had at least, ten lawsuits against him and the companies he worked for. Evidently, they tried to cover up his indiscretions.

"New man?" She smiled.

"Yes, my new man."

"Tell me about him." She stopped stirring the spaghetti noodles, wiped her hands on the apron and sat down. Anything to take the heat off my father. I just shook my head and started telling her about Courage.

"Well, I met him at the grocery store almost a year ago."

"A year? Why are you just now mentioning him?"

"You know me. I wanted to make sure he was the right one." I blushed discussing Courage.

"He must be if you're blushing."

"He's sweet, charming and..."

"And who the fuck cares? Why is this ungrateful bitch in my house?" My father busted in the kitchen. I didn't know he was home.

"Don't say that. She's your daughter."

"You mean the daughter who almost got me fired because she was being a whore?" I got up to leave.

"Now you wanna leave when someone talks about you not

being able to keep your legs closed." I tried my hardest to restrain myself from responding but it was hard with him ranting about the lies.

"People at the job talking about me bringing prostitutes to work now." He continued to rant.

"Goodbye."

"I'll walk you out." I could see my mom about to cry. My father has always been an asshole and it's sad to say, he loved his job and the people he worked with more than us.

His behavior towards me is nothing new. It's the reason Zakiya told me not to come here alone. She's witnessed his actions and almost fought him once. Crazy right? My friend fighting my father, but it almost happened.

"You're not going anywhere. The bitch can walk herself out."

BOOM! He pushed my mom into the refrigerator and the toaster fell on top of her head.

"Are you fucking crazy? Don't put your hands on my mother." I ran over and kneeled down in front of her.

"You ok?" The edge off the toaster must've hit her pretty hard because a gash appeared on the side of her head.

"I'll be ok."

"Ma... What the fuck?" I shouted when my hair was grabbed.

"Get the fuck out. I'll take care of my wife."

"I'm not leaving my mother."

WHAP! He backhanded me and the side of my eye split open.

"Stop it Larry. Don't touch her." My mom struggled to stand.

"You bastard." I pushed him into the wall and saw nothing but stars when he punched me in the face.

"I'm not going to tell you again. Get the fuck outta my house and don't come back." Blood was gushing out my nose and I could barely see with the blood coming down my eye.

"Mommy, come with me." She had her knees to her chest crying. This is the first time my father has ever put his hands on me. I can't say the same for my mother though. He's laid hands on her for as long as I can remember.

"Tell that bitch not to come back." My father ordered my mom to say. She shook her head no. He grabbed her by the hair.

"Tell her." His fingers were squeezing her face.

"Don't come back Andrina." He let go making my mom hit her face on the side of the cabinet.

I ran out the house holding my nose because the bleeding wouldn't stop and my father refused to let me get a paper towel or tissue. I hopped in my car and called Zakiya and she didn't answer. I continued wiping the blood and it was distracting me from driving. I didn't realize it, until the loud crashed stopped me from driving altogether. Courage is going to kill my father.

CHAPTER 19

Conscience

"What's up sis?" Consequence spoke into the phone.

"Hey. Where's Courage?"

"Right here. What's wrong? Why you sound upset?" I had a slight smile on my face when he asked. I loved my brothers to death an no matter what we went through, I'd always have their backs.

"I was driving... and.... um there was an accident."

"Shit. You ok? Where are you?" He started panicking and I could hear Courage in the background asking what happened.

"I'm fine. It wasn't me but..."

"But what?"

"Does Courage girlfriend drive a Hyundai; an older model?" He asked him and once he said yes, I knew it was about to be a problem.

My family knew about Andrina and were anticipating

meeting her. However, my mom would call Courage and say, I'm having a big dinner so bring her over. Before he could ask, Ciara would pop up. Instead of bringing any drama to the house my mom just said forget it. We weren't sure if the baby Ciara had is Courage's, and she didn't wanna upset her and make her possibly miscarriage.

Courage of course didn't give a fuck and said Andrina could hold her own. The same way Zakiya did with Lisa, which I still laugh about that. In the end, my mom said just wait and that she's going to stop by my brother's house to meet her this weekend. Not sure after what I saw, is it going to happen.

"Consequence, if this is the same car, someone ran a red light and hit her, then pulled off."

"Shit. Where you at?"

"Following the ambulance to the hospital."

"You sure it's her?" He asked.

"I wasn't until I got out the car and looked at her face. Bro, something happened to her before the accident."

"Why you say that?"

"Her entire face had blood on it, and she was hit on the passenger side. I know she may have hit her head but it was too much blood for it to just happen. Consequence, I was behind her car. It wouldn't have been that much blood already."

"Fuck! When you get there, tell them she's pregnant."

"Oh my God!"

"I know. We'll be there soon." I parked in the lot and ran as fast as I could with my big ass stomach. I was seven months now and you'd think I had twins coming.

"Hi. Can I help you?" The receptionist at the ER desk asked.

"Yes. My brothers girlfriend was brought in the ambulance." I pointed to them taking her out.

"I need to let the doctors know she's pregnant."

"Go right in and there's another desk. Let the nurses know and they'll go from there." I waited for her to press the button and walked in the back to do what she said. I spoke to the nurse and they let me follow them up to the labor and delivery floor. I sent a text to Courage and when I finished, my phone rang.

"Baby, are you ok? Where are you?" Rock asked in a panic.

"I'm ok. Courage's girlfriend was in a bad accident and she's pregnant."

"Damn."

"How'd you find out?" I hadn't even gotten the chance to tell him yet.

"Consequence called asking if I could find out who the hit and run driver is. He said you were there, and I panicked."

"Aww. Baby I'm ok. I'm gonna stay here until Courage gets here."

"Stay up there with them. I'll pick you up."

"Babe, I'm fine."

"I don't care Conscience. I know you're safe with them around. I'll be there to get you."

"Fine." We said, I love you to one another and disconnected the call.

"Hi. Are you with the lady who was brought in the ambulance?" The nurse asked. I missed the elevator with the people who brought her up because I was on the phone.

"Yes. Her boyfriend is on the way."

"They're taking her for a few x-rays and then she'll be placed in a room. The ER nurses stated she's expecting."

"Yes she is."

"Ok. You can wait in here because this is the room she'll be in."

"Thank you." She walked out and I took a seat in one of the chairs. What a way to meet? I called my mom and explained to her what went down. As we were talking Consequence and Courage walked in.

"Did they say anything?" I explained what the nurse told me.

"Where is she?" Zakiya ran in and stopped when she saw me and Consequence.

"They have her in X-ray." Courage said staring out the window.

"Do we know happened? Who did this to her?"

"If I knew yo ass was going to be a pain, I would've called you later. Why didn't you change your clothes first?"

"Don't start with me Consequence and why aren't you sitting down? You were shot and..." You could hear the concern in her voice.

"I'm fine Zakiya." She folded her arms across her chest.

"You better be. Had me all hot and bothered last night and not only did you not have condoms, you fell asleep on me." She tried to whisper but me and Courage heard and busted out laughing.

"You talk too much."

"You ashamed that you were with me last night and not the stalker bitch?" Consequence looked at me and I shook my head.

"You know what? Don't bring your ass over no more." She stormed out.

"Why you doing her like that bro? Both of y'all wanna be with each other." Courage told him.

"I'm no good for her. What if she does the same shit my ex do? Then I have to kill her and..."

"I would never do that Consequence." She overheard him talking when she came in to retrieve her things.

"It don't matter, Zakiya. We're not together and won't ever be. I like to fuck different women and you already said, you're not ok with it." If I didn't know any better, I'd say she was about to cry when she ran out. I wobbled out behind her and saw her at the other end of the hall wiping her face.

"He's so got damn mean for no reason. How does he expect me to love him when he acts this way?" Is she in love with my brother?

"He doesn't want you to love him because then it means, he'll have to love you back." I handed her a tissue I grabbed from the nurses' desk.

"Excuse me."

"Consequence is a complicated man and if you're wondering, yes he's been this way, his whole life. The one woman who was able to get him to let his guard down, did him dirty and he swore off ever getting into a new relationship."

"Wasn't he with Lisa?"

"Yes and no." I told her the truth.

"She's a loyal piece of pussy to him Zakiya; nothing more, nothing less." She sucked her teeth.

"It is, what it is."

"Ughhhh. I thought I could handle his bi-polar, aggressive ass but I can't. One minute he's affectionate and loving to me and then we get around people and he switches up." I nodded. My brother is crazy like that.

"Listen, I can tell you guys have a little bit of money; you're probably rich so I get why he's probably ashamed to be seen with me."

"He hasn't told you who he is?" I asked.

"No. I do know he got me suspended from work and then I saved lil Con, and he got me a promotion. He hasn't told me how it made it happened and I didn't ask." She shrugged. Consequence not telling her who we are, made me wonder if he's tryna feel her out to see if she's only with him for money.

"I'm not dressed in expensive clothes, I'm from the hood and definitely don't speak snobby." I chuckled.

"I'm serious. He's probably used to women who have as much money as him, if not more. I'm not them and I won't ever try to be. All I can give him is my love and attention and he doesn't want it."

"Zakiya, he's only going to do what you allow. If you're

really done with him, then be done with him. If he comes over, make him leave. Treat him the way he treats you." She laughed.

"Are you trying to get me killed?"

"Zakiya, truth be told, you should've been dead the first day he met you in Walmart."

"Huh?"

"The fact you're still breathing and around him, let's all of us know, you're someone he wants."

"I can't tell." She shook her head.

"And you won't until he feels like he wants you to." I patted her arm and headed back to the room with her behind.

"Where's Consequence?" I asked and I know she was wondering too.

"Who knows?" Just as he said that, the nurse wheeled Andrina in. Her eyes were closed, and she had monitors on, there was a bandage on her eye and brace on her nose too.

"Let me hook her up to the machines and I'll let you know how she's doing." The doctor spoke before we could ask questions.

I stood by Courage and Zakiya stayed out the way too. When they hooked her stomach up to the machine and the heartbeat could be heard, I swear my brother shed a tear. He must really love Andrina because it takes a lot for him and Consequence to show any emotion.

"Ok. She suffered a broken nose and her eye required seven stitches." The doctor said and turned to us.

"She hit that hard?" My brother asked.

"No which is why I'm concerned."

"No!" Zakiya questioned.

"She was hit on the passenger side and if anything, she should've banged her head on the window. It's a possibility her nose could've hit the steering wheel, but it wouldn't have broke it."

"What?" Courage yelled.

"I'm assuming something happened before the crash, but I can't be certain. Maybe she can tell us more when she wakes up."

"Is there anything else?" I asked.

"Oh yes. As you stated, she's pregnant; two and a half months to be exact. The left side of her body may bruise due to the impact of the crash but otherwise she's ok. I'm going to keep her overnight for observation." Courage thanked him and he left.

"When I find out who did this, I'm gonna make sure they never see the light of day again." Courage said to Andrina even though she was asleep. Consequence walked in and Zakiya sucked her teeth.

"I'm going to go. Can you tell her to call me when she wakes up? I don't care what time it is." Courage nodded and Zakiya kissed her forehead before grabbing her things to leave.

"Consequence." I called out to him. He was about to go after her.

"I never get in your business and I'm not tryin to."

"Why do I feel like you're about to?" I laughed.

"It's no secret that she likes you. We all can tell, and I know you can but you're confusing the hell outta her with your bipolar moments. She thinks you're ashamed of her." He turned his face up.

"What? That ain't it."

"Why haven't you told her who you are?" He leaned against the wall carefully.

"I wanted to make sure she wasn't tryna be with me for money."

"That's not the case. She knows we have some money because of our parents' house and the car you drive but she has no idea that the man she's falling for is a billionaire."

"Why should I tell her?"

"You don't have to. Shit, Rock knows we're rich, but he doesn't know how much money we have either. I'm just saying, you're keeping her in the dark about who you are and how you feel." I walked over to him.

"If you don't want her, then let her be." I left him standing outside Andrina's door thinking. I feel bad he's confused but he can't be taking women through it too. It's not right and as a woman myself, I know what it's like to be led on and it's not fun at all.

CHAPTER 20

Rock

"'ight. I'll be back."

"Where you going?" Conscience asked after I dropped her off. Her brother had me worried like a motherfucker when be said she called about an accident. I thought she was involved, and it took her a minute to answer her phone.

"I told you, your brother asked me to find out who hit Andrina."

"Do you know Zakiya?" I stopped at the door.

"Why you asking me about her?" I moved towards her in the living room.

"Because when I asked you before you brushed it off."

"Ok and? We weren't even discussing her this time and you bringing it up."

"It's just ironic how she was at the hospital for a while and you were supposed to pick me up, and you arrive after she leaves. What a coincidence?" I chuckled and sat across from her.

"I told you before, I don't know who she is. If you're asking, do I know a woman named Zakiya? Yes, but I don't know if it's the same person because I haven't seen her in years."

"You're saying it's a possibility you know her?" I shook my head.

"Have I ever given you reason to believe I'm cheating?" I stared at her.

"Well no."

"Then what's the sudden need to find out if I know her?"

"I just don't wanna run across any of your ex's again and deal with the same shit." I stood in front of her.

"Make this your last time asking me about another woman." I went to leave and her mouth started going.

"I'm just saying Rock. You think I need this stress? I don't want bitches saying they had my man. Why can't you tell me the truth?" She pushed me into the wall and started punching me in the back. I turned and snatched her wrists.

"I never cheated on you Conscience and I wouldn't. You were there for me when I couldn't deal with my brother passing, even though, we were a new couple. The baddest bitch couldn't get me to fuck because I love you too much." She tried to back up, but I kept her wrists in my hand.

"I know a lotta women from my past but you're focused on one woman, all because I'm not answering questions the way you think I should. Guess what Conscience? No answer is ever going to be good enough for you because deep down, you will always assume I'm cheating." I let go and picked up my keys.

"You and my child mean everything to me, and I couldn't fathom losing you." I shook my head as I stared at her crying.

"We are done Conscience." I spoke firmly so she knew I wasn't playing.

"What?"

"Over. Finished. Not getting back together; done."

"Rock."

"I can't take this shit and I'll be damned if I spend the rest of my life with an unhappy woman." I sat the black box on the table.

"I planned on asking you to be my wife tonight, but the accident happened, so I was doing it tomorrow." She started walking to me.

"On some real shit Conscience, you need help. I'm not sure if it's a mental or emotional thing going on with you but I'm not dealing with this forever. Call me when you go into labor."

"ROCK!" She shouted as I closed the door. I had to get outta here because if I tried to comfort her, I'd end up staying and she needs to deal with her issues.

* * *

"What up? Let me get two shots of Henney." Consequence said and took a seat next to me at the bar. I was at this hole in the wall tryna deal with leaving Conscience and her brother here next to me. What are the odds?

"Shit. What you doing here? Thanks." I said to him and the bartender after she passed me a shot.

"Probably the same thing you doing here." He took his shot and asked for another one, along with a drink.

"Doubt it. You ain't in no relationship." He laughed.

"From what Conscience says, neither are you." I shook my head.

"Let me find out she called you."

"Actually, she called my mother, who called me."

"I tried man, but your sister got some shit going on." I was being honest. One minute Conscience and I are good, then the next, she's flipping.

"The problem with Conscience is, she's spoiled." I looked at him.

"I'm not talking with materialistic items. I'm talking about with people. She's not used to anyone and when I say anyone, I mean anyone telling her no or not answering her directly."

"What?" I was shocked to hear they allowed her to be this way; especially him.

"She's the only girl and even though my mom tried to stop us from doing it, it never worked. My father is the number one culprit, then it's Courage and then me."

"I'm surprised you do it." He laughed.

"Trust me, I dig in her ass when she acts like a brat..." I cut him off.

"But you still do it."

"Eventually but not when she wants it done." We both shared a laugh.

"Anyway, the whole family told her you are the best thing that's ever happened to her."

"Thanks, I guess."

"Seriously. She used to deal with this other dude who was very good to her. He gave her whatever she wanted and let her be spoiled. We didn't know why, when Conscience would treat him like shit sometimes. Come to find out he didn't care because he had two other women he was dealing with. When she'd piss him off, he'd go to them until he felt like going back to her. They would make up, be fine for a few weeks and then, he'd leave."

"Oh." He turned to me.

"I'm not saying take her back because you know the type of nigga I am." I nodded.

The whole world knew who he was. He gave zero fucks about women and disrespected them whenever he felt like it. No idea why they still fucked with him, but they did. Bitches don't care where he is, they'll approach him and basically beg for him to fuck. It's crazy.

"If you don't wanna fuck with her, I got your back. All I ask is you don't neglect my niece or nephew."

"Never. Shit, I planned on asking her to marry me tonight, but the accident happened. I went to leave to see if I could find out more of what went down and she accused me of wanting some chick. I didn't answer her the way she expected, and I became a cheater and all types of shit. I'm not about to deal with that for the rest of my life. We can go-parent and that's it."

"I hear ya."

"I'm in these streets everyday making sure we live good. And before you say it, I know she has money but as a man, I'm not letting her take care of me." He agreed.

"I just wanna come home and lay up with my girl and not hear no shit." I asked the lady for another shot and handed him one.

"How did you even find me here?" He gave me a look.

"I know as many people as you, if not more." He's right.

All the street niggas knew them, and they are well respected. Being the Connect has its perks but being with a woman whose entire family basically owns the state of Florida does too.

Conscience never mentioned how much money she had, and I don't care. It wasn't until some dude who works for me, saw us out and asked if I were aware who she was. I told him no and he pulled up their name on the internet and I'll be damned. I was dating, or should I say in love with a damn billionaire.

I didn't think she had money because from what the internet said, her parents built the empire. However; each of them own properties and businesses here and in other parts of the country and world. I'm talking big companies that we'd never think black people could afford. She is the heiress of the family business and her brothers run it because their parents retired.

Anyway, her money isn't mine and I damn sure ain't about to live off no woman. Nor am I about to allow a spoiled billionaire to treat me like shit. I don't care if I was broke, ain't nobody tearing me down. I worked too hard to get where I'm at; whether my occupation legal or not.

"A'ight. Let me get outta here. I got my own personal issues to deal with."

"She got your head gone, huh?" He looked at me.

"Conscience told me some woman giving you a run for your money." He laughed.

"She is. I'll talk to you later and remember, she spoiled and if you don't wanna take her back, then don't. Just be there for my niece or nephew. You don't want your kid growing up without a parent and going through the same thing as lil Con." He patted me on the shoulder and left. I finished my drink and took my ass home.

CHAPTER 21

Courage

"How you feeling?" I asked Andrina when she opened her eyes. It was eight in the morning and a nigga hasn't been to sleep since the previous night. I was worried something would go wrong.

"I'm ok. I'm thirsty." I poured water in a cup, put a straw in and let her sip from it.

"Do you remember anything? The kind of car the person was driving or the persons face?" She nodded her head no.

"Can you help me in the bathroom?" I put the railing down and helped her up. I pressed the nurses' button because I took the monitors off her stomach.

"Is everything ok?" The nurse asked walking in.

"She needed the bathroom."

"Oh ok. Do you need anything?" I shook my head. Is she really tryna flirt?

"Bitch, really?" Andrina snapped.

"What?" She shrugged.

"You not about to have my wife all upset so take your dirty ass the fuck up outta here. If you come back, I'ma snap your got damn neck."

"Excuse me. Is that a threat?"

"Hold on Drina. Let me show this bitch." I left my girl in the bathroom and just as I approached the woman, my mom walked in.

"What's going on?"

"This man..." The nurse tried to speak, and my mom cut her off.

"You mean my son. Go ahead." My mom waited for her to respond but she left.

"The bitch tried flirting when I took Drina to the bathroom. Now she crying and..." I felt myself becoming upset for Drina.

"It's ok son. I'm going to have housekeeping come in to straighten up. Get her cleaned up and here are the things you asked me to bring." She handed me a bag and I walked in the bathroom. Drina was just finishing up.

"I can't believe he did this." She whispered.

"Who did this to you?" She jumped.

"Can you start the shower?" I turned it on and helped her get undressed. She only had bandages on her face so she could shower.

"Don't make me ask again." She started crying and took a seat on the hospital chair inside the shower.

"I can't help if you don't tell me."

"It's my problem Courage and I don't want you to kill him." I picked the soap up and tried my hardest to contain my anger.

"Kill who?"

"My father."

"Your father? Why would I kill him?" She broke down and told me the story of how she went to the house and her and her mom were discussing me. He arrived and attacked both of them.

"I won't kill him now Drina, but he has to see me." She looked up.

"Ain't no way in hell I'm ok with what he did to you. You could've died with all that blood leaking and he didn't give a fuck. The accident may have been avoided if you could see better."

"Courage please don't kill him. My mom will never forgive me, and I need her." I felt bad but she had to understand no one will put their hands on my woman.

"Need her for what? Didn't you say she stood there while your father put you out? And how he blames you for the shit at his job. I know you love your mom, but you don't need her." I lifted her head to look at me.

"You don't need no one who's not going to have your back. No one who can't and won't stand up to her husband knowing he's hurting their kid. And you damn sure don't need someone who's staying in a dangerous relationship. Drina, it's no telling how long he's been beating on her and I'm sorry, but I'm not letting my woman go over there and get caught up in their shit."

"I don't Courage." I rinsed the soap off.

"Did you or did you not get hit tryna help your mother?" She didn't respond.

"Exactly. He's toxic Drina and if your mom doesn't leave him, he's going to kill her."

"I know." I helped her out and wrapped the towel around her.

"How long has he been hitting her?"

"Years. This is the first time he's ever laid a hand on me."

"It'll be his last too." She wrapped her arms around me.

"I promise not to kill him but if he ever puts his hands on you again, he's a dead man." She nodded. I helped her get dressed and once we walked out, she stopped.

"Drina, this is my mom. Mom this is Drina."

"Gorgeous, Courage." Drina stared at me.

"You can't be talking about me with this brace on my face and bandages on my eye."

"Chile please. I've seen photos of you from my son." She turned to me.

"She's known about you for a while." I shrugged and helped her in the bed.

"Courage wanted me to meet you a couple months ago, and I wanted to keep the peace with his aggravating, possible baby mother."

"I understand."

"I apologize for putting her before you." My mom said and you could tell Drina was confused.

"Huh?"

"I knew my son was falling for you and he wanted us to meet. He didn't care about Ciara being there and usually I wouldn't either. However; I had to take into consideration that she may be having my grandchild. I can't have her under any stress and lose it. I would've never forgiven myself." Drina nodded.

"I'm sorry we're meeting under these circumstances, but I promise to be around more; especially now that you're expecting too. Are your parents happy?"

"They don't know." My mom looked at me.

"I'll let her tell you. I gotta make a run."

"Courage you promised." Drina yelled.

"I know. I'll be back." I kissed her and asked my mom not to leave until I returned.

****************************.

"Can I help you?" Drina's mom answered the door. She was a nice-looking older woman.

"I'm Courage. Where's your husband?" I moved right past her and started searching the downstairs.

"My husband?" She questioned and had a confused look on her face.

"Is he upstairs?"

"What's this about?" I used my hand to turn her head from side to side.

"He's not gonna stop." She snatched away.

"Who are you?" She asked again.

"Who the fuck are you?" The older black guy barked coming down the stairs.

"You must be Andrina's father."

"We don't have any kids." He spoke with finality.

"Damn. You'll disown your own daughter after putting hands on her?" I asked taking my phone out to show him a picture.

"This is what you did to my girl; your daughter." I showed him the phone and he smacked it out my hand.

"Oh, you tough?" I picked it up.

"Get out my house."

"Oh, I'm leaving. Right after I do this." I hooked off, catching him on the side of his face. He was dazed for a second. I continued hitting him over and over until I heard my brothers voice. He stayed in the car, but I guess I took too long.

"Oh my God!" Drina's mom yelled when she noticed the machete Consequence handed me.

"This is to make sure you never lay hands on my girl again." I chopped his right hand off.

"I'm gonna leave you with the left hand so you can get dressed. But let me hear you putting hands on your wife again and the other one's gone." By now he was half dead and going in and outta consciousness. I walked over to Drina's mom.

"This is your chance to leave. I'd take it if I were you." She nodded and wiped her eyes.

"I don't have anywhere to go."

"I thought you'd say that, so I booked you a room at this hotel." I gave her the name and address to it.

"They're aware you're coming. Someone will be there tomorrow to bring you clothes and anything else you need."

"Why are you helping me?"

"I'm not helping you. Your daughter is. As her man, I have to make sure my child's grandmother is here to see him or her born." She covered her mouth.

"Take what you need for tonight and in the morning. Don't worry about anything else."

"What about him?"

"Do you wanna leave him for good?" She shook her head yes.

"Then don't worry about anything else." She hugged me, ran upstairs and grabbed what she needed. She was back down in less than five minutes.

"I called 911 and said he tried to kill himself."

"I'm not worried. Let's go." She got in her car and sped out the driveway.

"Damn. She not playing." Consequence said as I picked up the machete and placed it in a bag.

"This isn't the first time she's left Drina said." I told him.

"Really?"

"Nah. She's left a few times. He calls, makes her feel bad and she's right back home." He shook his head.

"She better stay away this time because his ass may kill her for opening the door for you." He joked.

"I did my part. As long as he doesn't lay hands on Drina, I'm good."

"Drop me off at Zakiya's job." He said and I gave him a crazy look.

"I guess it's about time to settle down." He started laughing.

"What about Lisa?"

"I'll miss fucking her because Zakiya ain't about to let me do that, but the way Zakiya sex game set up, it's worth the loss."

"A'ight bro. Just remember she's not Lauren and I think she's too scared to cheat." We both shared a laugh.

"She better be." I dropped him off and went back to the hospital. I hope Drina's mom stay away because I'm not saving her again.

CHAPTER 22

Zakiya

KNOCK! KNOCK! I heard at my office door.

"Can I come in?" I rolled my eyes. I hadn't seen him since Andrina was in the hospital. I heard he stopped by the job and I wasn't here. I'm glad I wasn't but he caught me today.

"If I said no, you'd come in anyway."

"You're right." Consequence closed the door and I heard the lock click.

"Why you lock the door?"

"We need to talk."

"I seriously doubt the two of us have anything to discuss. How did you know I was here? Today is my day off as you can tell by my clothes." I had on a pair of jeans with a thin sweater and sneakers. I only came to grab some papers and do some work from home.

"What?" I turned my chair to face him. He was leaning on the window staring at me. I hated how attracted I am to him.

"Pussy wet?" I turned my chair back around and two seconds later, I was lifted out of it. He had my back against the window.

"I know its wet because my dick hard." He put my hand in his jeans and sure enough.

"Consequence, why are you..." He unbuttoned my jeans and removed them, along with my sneakers and panties.

"Come here." He sat in the chair stroking himself. I was so turned on, I placed myself in front of him and started playing in my pussy.

"You make some sexy ass faces when you about to cum." He stopped doing himself, moved closer to the desk and went head-first in between my legs.

"Right there baby. Yes." I came right away.

"You missed this dick, didn't you?" He wiped his mouth, slid me off the desk and onto him. When we became one, both of us moaned in delight.

"You feel so good Consequence." I tossed my head back and went up and down as he sat on the chair.

SMACK! Each time he smacked my ass, the urge to cum harder was right there.

"You tryna be my woman?" I stopped and stared at him.

"Are you serious?" He stood with me in his arms.

"I'm not gonna ask again. It's yes or no?" He placed my back against the window and maneuvered in and out slow.

"Yes baby. Oh gawd yes. Fuck me harder Consequence."

Why did I say that? He dug so deep inside; I lost my breath for a second. I never felt pain and pleasure such as this in my whole life. I came so hard; my body shook violently and that's never happened with anyone but him.

"This pussy talking to me Za. Fuck." He let me down, turned me around and placed both of my hands on the window. I literally could see Miami as I was getting fucked.

"What if someone sees us? Shittttt." He was finding places I didn't even know existed.

"Who cares? You're mine and I'm yours now. This my woman office and I'll fuck her in here anytime I want." I smiled and looked over my shoulder.

"You like hearing me say that huh?" He pulled me up by the hair and wrapped his hand around my throat. His dick was still going in and out.

"Don't cheat on me Consequence." He squeezed my neck tighter.

"Same goes for you because no matter how good this pussy is, I'll fucking kill you." He went faster and second later he exploded inside me.

"Always good Za." He smacked me on the ass and walked to the bathroom. I laid on the floor tryna catch my breath.

"Come here Za."

"I can't walk Consequence." He stood at the bathroom door grinning.

"Then crawl to me." I smirked.

"You wanna be nasty in here?" I asked and seductively crawled towards him. His hand was massaging his manhood.

"Suck my dick Za." I loved hearing him talk dirty.

"Make it real nasty and sexy." I made it over and stared up at him.

"I'm not gonna hurt you Za. It's as hard for me to trust, as it is you." I nodded and took him in my mouth. I gave my man all that I had in this office with no regrets.

"Here." He walked over to me after we got dressed.

"What's that?" He passed me a black bag.

"At least I don't have to get it." I opened the plan b and took the first pill.

"I knew I was running in this good ass pussy raw and wasn't pulling out." I laughed.

"Well, we gotta work on that. This is new and we don't need any kids." He wrapped his arms around me.

"When I want you to have my kids, won't be know plan b's available."

"Consequence, we..." He shushed me by putting his mouth on mine.

"Come on. My woman needs to shower."

"I washed up babe." He smiled when I called him that.

"Yea, but my nut is gonna keep dropping out." I busted out laughing. He held my hand in his and we stepped on and off the elevator together. All the staff were staring. I left the hotel with my man and nobody could tell me shit right now.

"Don't be getting all excited and shit when you see my house." Consequence joked. It's been a month since we've been a couple and actually, it's been good.

He's been at my house every night and so has lil Con. Rage, damn near kidnapped Andrina so when his son stays, he sleeps in Andrina's room. Lil Con loves it because he has me doing exactly what he wanted. I tucked him in at night and a few times, I let Consequence sleep and took him to school. It made me happy to see how excited he was to have a woman in his life. He has his family and nana, but I definitely understand the difference.

"Whatever. It better be all that." Just as I said it, he stopped at a gate, pressed a few buttons and it opened. All you could see is a long driveway and beautiful landscaping on both sides.

"Oh my gawd. Is that your house?" I was in awe of the size. It literally looked like it could be two football fields. Most of it is made out of glass and that's just from the front.

"Damn. If you that excited, wait til you see the inside." He drove around the circular area and parked in front of the door.

"You not getting out?" He asked and I folded my arms.

"You not opening the door?"

"You becoming spoiled already and you only got the dick." He always talking shit. I bet he opened the door tho.

"I have the dick, the man, and now the key to your house." I held it up. He gave it to me last night and said we not staying at my place all the time and he'll want me here.

"I may have to reevaluate things. You got a key fast." He tried to snatch it out my hand.

"Nope." I ran to the door and when it opened, amazed isn't even the word for how it looked. I swore we were in a magazine house.

"Is that the beach?" I pointed to a window on the opposite side of the house. I thought only the front of the house was made of glass, but it's the entire place.

"Yes." I opened the door and walked around the pool. He lived on a hill and in order to get to the beach you would've had to drive. Plus, it had a humongous gate around it.

"How do you get down there?"

"I usually take the walk. It gives me time to think."

"Is it private? I mean do you see people?"

"Yes. It's very private. As you can see." He waved his hand around.

"All of these houses are big. This specific part of the beach, is away from the spot everyone goes to." He held me in front of him.

"You and lil Con really have it made."

"We do but he's still losing out on having a mother." He kissed the side of my neck and led me back in the house.

"Do you think she'll ever return?" He closed the door.

"To be honest Za, if she did, I'm not sure I want her to meet him."

"Can I ask why?"

"I'm afraid, she'll leave again, and he won't take it as well, being that he's older."

"I understand."

"Let me show you the rest of the house." He took me room to room, and I couldn't tell you which one I loved more.

"This bed is big as heck." We were in the master bedroom. It had a balcony overlooking the beach too.

"It's basically two California kings' put together."

"Good. When you make me angry, you can be on one side, and I'll be on the other." He walked over to me.

"Yea right. Yo ass going in a room down the hall."

"I'm the guest and you're supposed to be nice to all your guests." He lifted me up.

"Guest? Nah, if you play your cards right, you'll be the woman of the house." I leaned down and kissed him.

"I wanna fuck you in the pool." He put me down.

"Ok." I felt like a high school kid with a crush on the most popular guy there.

"You tryna stay the night?" He asked on the way to the pool.

"Do I have a choice?"

"Not really." I laughed and joined my man in the pool. We about to christen this entire house.

CHAPTER 23

Lisa

"I told you to leave him alone Lisa." I was at Conscience house hoping Consequence stopped by. I hadn't seen him in over a month.

"You know how your brother and I are. You think he messing with someone else?" She stopped moving around the kitchen.

"Look, I'm not telling my brothers business. If you wanna know anything, you'll have to ask."

"That means he is. Who is she?" She shook her head.

"All I'm going to say is, if he wants you, he'll call."

"Its that hood bitch, right? I've seen him with her around town." She shook her head.

SLAM! The front door closed and both of us walked out the kitchen to see who it was.

"Rock? What are you doing here? Is everything ok?" I think

both of us were shocked to see him. I knew they were broken up over her being a brat. He went to the last doctor appointment from what she says and left right after he said her and the baby were ok.

"We need to talk."

"Ummm ok. Lisa can you turn the oven off? The food is done." I told her yes and pulled the lasagna out. Tonight, we were supposed to have girl's night and as of right now, it's just me.

As I closed the oven door, I heard someone coming in. I went to check and stopped short as Consequence typed away on his phone. He was so damn sexy and all I wanted to do is let him fuck me to sleep.

He wore dark denim jeans with a crisp white T and Jordan's to match. Those were his favorite sneakers and he looked damn good in them if I must say so myself. The waves in his hair were perfect and I couldn't help but bite down on my lip thinking about the last time we were together.

"Tha fuck you doing here?" He barked taking me out my thoughts.

"Conscience and I are having a girls night. She made lasagna. You want some?"

"I'm good. Where she at?" He glanced around the house.

"Rock just got here. They upstairs talking."

"A'ight." He went to leave, and I jumped in front of him.

"Move Lisa."

"What's wrong? Why haven't you been answering my calls or letting me see you?" I kept blocking the door.

"You sound desperate as fuck right now." He moved me over.

"I'm always gonna be desperate for you." I removed my shirt and undid my bra.

"You bugging." He said.

"Am I?" I started taking my jeans and panties off. I knew this wasn't my house and Conscience would kill me if she saw me like this, but Consequence is right. I'm desperate. Desperate for him and I'll do anything to make him see we belong together.

"If I'm bugging, why is my friend here tryna bust out your jeans?" I unzipped his pants and pulled it out.

"Yea. I love seeing this thick vein pop up when I'm about to suck you off." He stared down at me get in a squatting position.

"Mmmm. You still taste good baby." I deep throated him and bobbed up and down for what felt like forever.

"Let me taste you daddy." When I said that, he came.

"Put your clothes on before Conscience sees you." He gathered himself.

"Why don't you help me." I grabbed my things and headed to the downstairs bathroom naked, with him following." Men are like sick puppies when their dick hard. He closed the door behind him, I dropped my stuff and started giving him a hand job. I let the tip touch the top of my pussy and slid it up and down so he could feel how wet I was.

"I don't have any condoms."

"You can pull out." I turned, bent over and pushed myself on him. He stood there not moving.

"It's ok. I got this." He grabbed my hips and started pounding into me. Once our eyes met in the mirror, he stopped, pulled out and left me naked and confused. I rushed to put my clothes on, came out and saw him walking out the front door.

"What the hell?" Conscience said coming down the stairs and Rock was behind her shaking his head. I didn't care what either of them thought of me.

"Why are you chasing after my brother?" I didn't answer and ran out.

"Consequence? Why did you leave?" He got in his car and pulled off. I turned and saw Conscience standing there with her arms folded.

"You have to go."

"What?" I asked going inside to grab my things.

"You tried to seduce my brother even after I told you he had a woman."

"Tried to? Ha! I had him." She covered her mouth.

"What? We've been sleeping together for years. Did you honestly think some new chick would stop us?"

"Lisa. Why don't you want him to be happy?"

"He won't be happy with anyone but me." I shrugged and walked out her house.

"Oh, and tell your new friend, the Zakiya bitch. She'll never have him to herself. Matter of fact, I'll go tell her myself." I sat in my car and drove to my next destination.

* * *

"Hi. I'm looking for someone named Zakiya." I said to the woman at the front desk. I couldn't come last night because it was a little late and when I called, they said she wouldn't be in until today. I took my time getting here just in case he showed up.

"She just went to the cafeteria for her lunch break. You want to wait or..." I cut the little bitch off.

"No. I know where the cafeteria is." I left her standing there and went straight there. I've been here a few times with Consequence for him to pick things up. He always had me wait in there or one of the conference rooms.

When I opened the door, it was only a few people there. She sat alone pulling things out from a lunch bag. I hated how pretty she was, and she wasn't even trying. Her hair was done nicely, and her uniform looked perfectly pressed.

It wasn't the regular dress/apron looking one the housekeepers wore either. No, she had on khaki pants with a polo shirt that had the hotel logo on it. I know this bitch didn't get a promotion.

"Zakiya." She looked up and sucked her teeth.

"As you can see, I'm trying to enjoy my lunch." She continued pulling out the soda and chips.

"How can I help you Lisa?" She unwrapped her sandwich.

"May I?" I pointed to the seat across from her.

"It's obvious you have some things on your mind so go ahead." She took a bite of her sandwich.

"For starters, I would like to say that I'm fully aware of you and Consequence's relationship."

"How so?" She didn't deny it.

"I've seen the two of you around and whenever he stops fucking me, it means he found someone."

"Ok. What else?"

"Welllllll." I dragged the word out with a grin on my face.

"I just wanted to tell you we've been sleeping together..." She cut me off.

"For years; I know. Keep going." Is this bitch rushing me?

"Oh, he told you?"

"Yup."

"Did he tell you about last night?" She laughed.

"He was with me last night Lisa. He's been with me every night if you wanna be technical." She gave me a fake smile.

"I don't know what time he got to you last night, but we were very cozy at his sisters house."

"He wasn't there longer than twenty minutes." I laughed.

"Is that what he told you?"

"I don't have a reason not to trust him Lisa. Whatever it is you wanna tell me, just say it."

"He and I, did some things at his sister's house..." I glanced around the room and whispered.

"We were very naughty, and I must say, we both enjoyed every minute with each other."

"Anything else?" I could see the sadness on her face and hear the hurt in her voice.

"Nope." I pushed the chair out and stood.

"If I can still sleep with him when he's married, I can continue when he has a new chick." I blew her a kiss and walked out the door.

"LISA!" I stopped. She caught me right outside the door. No one was out here.

"Do you have your phone on you?"

"Yes, I do." I handed it to her.

"I want you to call Consequence and put him on speaker." I dialed his number and did like she asked.

"What Lisa?"

"Consequence, did you fuck her last night and then come to my house?"

"Za?"

"Za?" He giving her nicknames now. I thought to myself.

"This bitch brought her disrespectful ass to my job, to fill me in on your little rendezvous last night. So, I'm going to ask you again. Did you fuck her last night and come to me?"

"I went home and showered first. Za, listen." She walked back in the cafeteria.

"She left." I told him and walked towards the front of the hotel.

"Why the fuck did you go to her job?"

"I'm tired of you playing me out for these women. They need to know you and I will always be a thing. Fuck their feelings." The phone disconnected. Zakiya stormed out the cafeteria and handed me something.

"What's this?"

"The key to his house. You can have it; you can have him

and this job. I quit." She going off and I'm stuck on the fact he gave her a key to his house. I barely get a key to the hotels we stay in.

"Ok but I definitely don't need this job." I walked out with my head held high. Job well done.

CHAPTER 24
Consequence

"I'm gonna kill that bitch." I said to Rage who was sitting next to me when Lisa called. I thought it was her anyway.

"What happened?"

"I fucked up."

"Fucked up how? There she is." He pointed to the woman walking in her shop.

We left for Tampa early this morning to catch this bitch. She's the woman who dated the guy Carlos, who I still hadn't murdered yet. He's locked away being tortured for information which he refuses to give up. Snatching his girl up may change his mind.

She was a pretty woman with what appeared to be a purchased body. I'm not knocking women who get surgery because their bodies look good. Lauren had it done, and the shit made me wonder why she needed it when her body was already nice.

When she told me, it made her feel better about herself, I knew she had a lot of insecurities for some reason. Come to find out, a lot of these women do, which is why they have it done.

Anyway, Zakiya on the other hand doesn't have a bit of anything done to her body and I love that shit. She's what I thought I had in Lauren and I already fucked up messing with Lisa. I don't even know why I let it go down that way, knowing she can't fuck with Zakiya sexually on any level. Seeing her naked made me brick up and like a dummy, I fell right into her trap. I didn't know she would go to Zakiya's job. Now, it's some more shit I'll have to smooth over when we return.

"I went over Cee house last night to ask about Rock knowing Zakiya. She mentioned something about thinking they were a couple previously and how she doesn't want it to interfere with the two of them."

"I thought her and Rock broke up." Rage questioned.

"Oh, he left her spoiled ass for sure, but he was there last night." He shook his head.

"I get there and Cee upstairs talking to him and Lisa asks why I haven't been answering her calls."

"And?" He asked. I ran my hand over the top of my head.

"And she stripped. Man, she pulled my dick out and started giving me head. I thought Cee was gonna come down, so I thought of it being Zakiya and came fast."

"Then you left right?"

"I followed her in the bathroom and fucked her."

"What?" He all but shouted.

"Yea. Once I looked at her in the mirror, I pulled out and left her there. She started yelling about me leaving her and chased me out the house. I bounced, went home to shower and then back to Zakiya house."

"Tell me you didn't fuck her."

"Nah. It's that time of month for her. I was happy too because Zakiya loves to fuck."

"Listen. If you plan on staying with Zakiya, not only are you gonna have to beg and plead for her to take you back, because we all know she ain't having it." I nodded.

"You're gonna have to do something about Lisa."

"I already know. Let's go." We got out the car and walked up to the woman who was engaged in a conversation with someone else.

"Damn. Y'all both fine. Where the hell you from?" I instantly thought of Zakiya when she had the same reaction upon seeing me the first time.

"What's up? Can we talk to you real quick?" The woman we were there for caught an attitude.

"I have work to do and...." I yoked her up.

"Bitch, did we ask what you had to do. Yo! Come get this other bitch." I shouted to Ron and John who were in a black van.

"Rage make sure no one is in the shop and lock it up."

"What the hell?"

"Shut the fuck up." The black van pulled up and John hopped out.

"Please don't. I didn't see anything." The other woman yelled out.

"The fact you're even saying that, is a reason we taking yo ass." John threw her in the van hard as hell and I tossed the other one.

"We good." Rage said and pulled the gate back down to her shop.

"Let's ride." I said and all of us drove back to Miami after making two other stops.

I let Rage drive so I could rest my eyes for a few. I did try and call Zakiya a few times and it kept going go voicemail. I knew she was with Andrina because my brother told me. I'll deal with her later.

* * *

"WAKE UP MOTHERFUCKER!" I punched Carlos in the face and his eyes shot open.

"I have a surprise for you." I taunted.

"Fuck you."

"It's good to know your family wasn't worth shit." Rage said behind him.

"What?" He started panicking.

"Yea. I picked your bitch up this morning and your mom. She wasn't too fond of us barging in on her sucking some old man dick but hey, when you need to speak to someone, you have to barge in."

"My mother? What did you do?" I walked over to the box on the table and brought it over to him.

"Is the crate ready?" I asked Rage who had some of the workers opening the doors.

"Your mom wasn't happy you put her in your bullshit. She took her death like a champ tho." I opened the box in front of him to reveal her head and he vomited all over himself.

"You thought snatching my son wasn't gonna have repercussions? My name is Consequence, duh? It describes the type of man I am when dealing with people. People who underestimate me because I'm not some big-time drug dealer or hang in the streets." I dropped the box at his feet and turned him around.

"Yo! What the fuck?"

"Your woman or should I say wife; and her loud mouth sister." We found out their relation as they cried in the back of the van. John said all they kept saying was, their mom would be upset and searching for them."

"They didn't know how to respect me and my brother." I pointed to Rage standing there with the blowtorch in his hand.

"We only wanted to ask some questions and your wife here, had a smart-ass mouth and as you can see, she wrote a check her ass couldn't cash." Rage barked.

"Make sure each crate has enough charcoal under it." I told Ron who stood next to them.

"Carlos, what you see here is three boxed crates. One holding your wife, her sister and their mother. Underneath each one, is a pile of charcoal doused with lighter fluid. Each time you don't answer a question, Rage is going to light the torch, which will ignite the fire and burn them inside the crate."

"CARLOS WHAT DID YOU DO?" His wife cried and you could see the crate moving. They were hung from the ceiling and low enough to the ground for the fire to be felt.

"Tell me what you want man?" I stood in front of him.

"You know what I want. Why did you not only pull a gun on my five-year-old son, you tried to take him. Why?" He didn't answer.

"Light them up." You heard the torch go on and we watched the fire shoot into the crate. His wife was jumping up and down inside as the flames went through.

"I wouldn't do that if I were you." Rage taunted the three women.

"The more you jump, the worse you're making it. If the bottom cracks, you fall out and burn faster." She stopped moving.

"Each one will go through this until you tell me what I wanna know."

"Ok. The guy who hired me knows you're not from the streets. It's why he paid me to try and take your son. When it didn't happen, I was already paid which is why I had the money at the club."

"Keep going." I waved my finger in a circle for him to continue.

"It's not him calling the shots."

"What?" Rage asked.

"It's someone else. He's just the one who has the money to pay out to make it happen."

"Who's the other person?"

"I don't know." I nodded my head to Rage, and he lit his wife up again.

"Please. That's all I know. Let my wife go. I'll take whatever consequence it is for her." He cried out.

"Where can I find these people?"

"I don't know that either. All I know is, the guy mentioned coming here when you least expect it and when he does, all that's gonna be left are your ashes."

"Damn, somebody really tryna kill me." I joked.

"Can you let them go?" He pleaded for their lives again.

"Can't do it. They've seen and heard too much. Do your thing brother." Rage smirked and sprayed the flame from the blowtorch inside each crate. It didn't take long for them to burn because Ron squirted the lifted fluid in the crate before Rage lit them up. All you heard was screaming and soon after the smell came.

"Get this cleaned up and well reconvene tomorrow. If someone is coming for me, I need to be ready from every angle." I walked out and drove home. I planned on seeing Zakiya but what happened is still fresh, I'll give her a few days.

CHAPTER 25

Courage

"Umm."

"Umm what bitch? Tha fuck you call me over here for?" I barked at Ciara who was six months and getting on my nerves.

"The mortgage is due and so are the utilities. I don't have food and…"

"And what?"

"I don't understand why you're so angry with me. Ok, you didn't strap up and now I'm pregnant. We have to deal with it but why you keep snapping on me?"

"Why you think I'm snapping? You calling and texting me all hours of the night with bullshit knowing I'm with my girl. You don't even want shit at that." I barked.

"I'm sorry for wanting my baby father to be here when our child kicks."

"Don't use no fake ass reverse psychology on me. I told you

to terminate the baby, you didn't and now we have to deal with it. You thought it would make me continue fucking you." I moved closer to her.

"You don't ever have to worry about my child being taken care of because if the baby is mine, I will be around. What I won't do, is fuck or take care of you."

"Oh, but you can take care of her?" I laughed.

"You know what's crazy? She won't let me do a damn thing for her. Nothing. I can't even buy her take out half the time because she doesn't wanna become dependent on me. But you..." I looked her up and down.

"You want me to give, give and give, while you do nothing. Yo ass don't work, clean, cook or even have a fucking hobby and why is that?" She didn't say anything.

"Because I do all that for you. You have a chef, housekeeper, and money in your account. I pay all the bills and you still not satisfied. What the fuck do you want from me?" I felt myself getting angry.

"I want us to be together Courage."

"Stop the shit, Ciara. The problem is you didn't want me and now that I moved on and you can't get no more dick, you wanna be back in my life, right?" She was quiet.

"When Andrina wasn't around and I was dropping dick off, you were good. There wasn't any pressure on us being together." I made my way to the door.

"I've gone to every doctor appointment with you and had all the baby items you wanted, delivered and put together."

"Rage this baby should have both parents."

"The baby will have both of us. We just won't live in the same house. I suggest you get on board because I'll have no problem taking the child and raising it with my new girl."

"Like hell you will."

"Then get it together Ciara. Find a man to keep you warm at night. Get a job, find a hobby or something. Leave me the fuck alone unless it's about the baby." I opened the door.

"And don't call me over with any more bullshit about the bills being due. You know my mother handles all that." I slammed the door and went to my car. I could see now she's going to be worse when the baby comes. I need to talk to Andrina because we may need to take the baby.

* * *

"Hello Courage." Andrina's mom spoke as she sat in the living room. My girl said her mom contacted her and asked to see her. I wasn't letting her come to my crib.

"Hey." I kissed Andrina on the cheek and went in her room. I grabbed a towel, and my hygiene stuff and walked in the bathroom.

If Zakiya wasn't here, I'd come out in my towel but it's not the case. Andrina told me she's been locked in her room since the situation happened with Consequence. I understand he comfortable with Lisa but he gotta let her go if he plans on being with anyone.

"No mommy. Why would you do that?" I heard as I finished getting dressed in the bathroom. It wasn't my concern unless my girl called me in. I picked my stuff up and made sure I didn't leave anything in here and walked back to her room.

"Courage, can you come in here?" I put my slides on and went to see what happened.

"What up?" Andrina looked at me and took another look before smirking. I mouthed, *I got you later.*

"My mom here, decided to go back to my dad." I shrugged my shoulders.

"Babe, it's not safe for her." She followed me in the kitchen.

"Drina, what's he gonna do with one hand? He probably needs her to help now that he's handicapped." I chuckled thinking about the time I saw him after it happened.

He was getting out a cab and his arm was covered but I couldn't see his hand coming out the sleeve. It's what he gets for touching my girl. I don't care what happened to her mom but when it comes to Drina, no one will touch her.

"I don't want her to go back. I feel like it's a trick. What if he tries to kill her for it?"

"Then she'll be dead."

"COURAGE!" She popped me on the arm, and I grabbed her waist.

"Andrina, my mother always taught us, people will only do what they're allowed. It's fucked up that she wants to return; it is. However, she's grown and can make her own decisions."

"But..."

"But you tried to help, and I put her up in a hotel to keep him away. Babe, he's all she knows and vice versa. If she wants him to go upside her head, then it's her choice."

"I'm scared he's going to hurt her."

"Again, if she's taking the risk, then she'll have to deal with the repercussions. All you can do is be there for her."

"I can't go over there."

"Hell no you can't. If he even got smart with you because you stopped by, I'd have to kill him, and you'll be mad at me. Ain't nobody got time for that. So keep yo ass away and if you two want to see one another, pick a spot."

"I guess you're right. I love you Courage. You always know what to say." I put my face in her neck.

"When she leaves, I'm gonna know what to do too." She laughed and walked back in the living room. I grabbed a water and went in her room.

"So you're gonna stay with him after he cut your fathers hand off?" I heard as my foot hit the threshold. After all I did to help this bitch, she got the nerve to pop shit.

"I don't know what you're talking about mommy. Courage was with me when it happened, and I don't appreciate you accusing him." I smiled at my girl taking up for me.

"I watched him do it."

"Goodbye mother. I will not sit here and let you make accusations up about him. Are you trying to send him to jail? Because if anyone should be in jail, it should be my father; your husband. Remember, he backhanded me so hard, he split my eye. Then he broke my nose because I was protecting you." Her mom said nothing.

"Exactly. You wanna say my man did something horrible to

my father but don't wanna discuss what your husband did to me. Goodbye." Andrina opened the front door.

"Andrina."

"I hope and pray your foolishness of going back doesn't get you killed." Her mom put her head down. The door slammed and I walked over to Drina.

"She's gonna be good." I tried to say comforting words.

"You think so?"

"Hell no. Soon as he gets enough strength, he's gonna beat her ass again." She laughed.

"Let me make you feel better." I locked the front door and led her in the bedroom.

"Make sure you don't yell." I told her. My girl needed to be taken outta her funk and I'm just the one to do it.

CHAPTER 26

Zakiya

"I can't believe you quit. Why would you do that?" Drina asked as we sat outside the restaurant having lunch.

"I didn't want to sis but come on. I would've rather stayed as just the housekeeper. He's the one who offered me a higher position."

"True but you were making great money. How can we afford to pay rent?"

"Girl, I can get a job anywhere." She snickered.

"Not unless you wanna work under him again." We heard and turned around to see Conscience. Her stomach was huge, and she still looked beautiful.

"Excuse me." I said.

"Do you mind if I sit?" She asked and both of us shrugged. Some guard pulled the chair out for her.

"Can I have a strawberry lemonade and a Caesar salad with no croutons?" She asked the waitress who rushed to get it.

"The bitch wasn't that fast when we ordered." Conscience chuckled.

"When you're the owner, they'll do everything a lot faster."

"OWNER?" Me and Andrina shouted. Conscience smiled and accepted her salad and drink.

"I know you ladies don't know much about me and my family so let me fill you in on a little."

"You can inform Andrina because she's about to have your niece or nephew, bonding y'all for life." I stood and tossed my napkin on the table.

"I'm done with Consequence." I picked up my purse.

"Sit down Zakiya." She barked.

"What?"

"You heard me. Sit down." She stabbed her salad and put the fork in her mouth.

"You don't tell me what to do." I snapped.

"Listen Zakiya, you are a great fighter but in no means to disrespect, you won't get a win over here."

"Who the fuck you talking to?"

"Zakiya please. Why are you snapping on her when she's only here to talk? I swear, Consequence got you mad at the world." Drina said pissing me off. His sister didn't need to know our business.

"Really?"

"I'm serious Zakiya. We didn't hurt you and I get it; he messed up but damn. She's only talking." I sucked my teeth and sat down.

"You have five minutes and I'm out." Conscience chuckled.

"You'll stay here as long as I want you to. If you have a problem with that, blame it on my brother. You should've never gotten involved with Consequence."

"You don't have to tell me. It's a mistake I won't make again."

"Zakiya Summers, you have the same attitude as I, which is why I find your nastiness funny. I can see how people view me when I respond the way you are." I rolled my eyes.

"Anything else, Miss Waters?" The waitress asked as she took away the salad.

"Yes. I'll have a rib eye steak, well done with mashed potatoes and a skewer of grilled shrimp on the side."

"Right away." She hurried off.

"Look, my brother likes you; a lot actually." I rolled my eyes.

"I doubt it. If he did, he'd be able to control his dick." I drank some of the water still left on the table.

"I agree and both me and my mother dug in his ass yesterday."

"Why is that?"

"For starters... He gave you a key to his house." She took a sip of her drink.

"Shit, as long as he fucked Lisa, she's never received a kiss from him, let alone a key."

"A kiss?" Andrina questioned, which made me curious.

"I'm sure when they were young he may have, but my brother has a no kissing rule if you're not his woman. I know firsthand, that he's never kissed Lisa after he turned eighteen."

"Whattttttt?" Me and Andrina couldn't believe it.

"Nope. He said, kissing brings on emotions and he knew, him and Lisa would never be a couple and its no need to confuse things with her or any other woman." I smiled on the inside because he and I loved kissing one another. Does that mean he loves me?

"He's never shown her off or taken her on dates. Lauren is the only woman he's done that with and now you."

"Should I feel honored?"

"Any man who shows his woman off isn't to make her feel good about herself. It's to show his appreciation of who he's with. To show her, outta all the women in the world, he picked her. And to show her, he's willing to give her anything to make sure she's happy." I didn't say anything.

"What Lisa did is fucked up on all levels and I'm surprised you didn't beat her ass."

"I would never show my weakness to her." I thought back to the night Consequence told me not to let her see me cry.

I saw the satisfaction on her face as she told me about their indiscretion. I held it in and cried my eyes out in the office. I already fell for him and it hurt to hear he gave himself to someone else. So what he was with her for years. It was supposed to be me and him against the world.

"Consequence was happy you didn't because she'd play off it but let me tell you something about Lisa." I made myself comfortable. I guess listening to her isn't so bad.

"Lisa used to be our neighbor growing up. Her and Consequence shared things and have for years. He's never gotten serious with any woman besides Lauren and even then, something was lacking because he still fell victim to Lisa."

"Oh, I must be lacking something because he ran back to her." I sassed.

"To be honest, I thought that too." She gave me a fake smile.

"Then, I pulled my brother to the side and asked him privately what is it that keeps him in bed with Lisa and you know what he said?"

"I don't think I wanna know."

"Shit, I do. What he say?" Drina was all excited.

"Really?"

"Hell yea really? This is like a damn soap opera." She said making us laugh.

"He said, she's the only one who hasn't let him down."

"I'm confused."

"Consequence has had plenty of women growing up and each one never measured up to the woman he was looking for. They couldn't handle him sexually, mentally or emotionally. Then, Lauren came along and broke him down, only to break his heart so what did he do? Went back to fucking Lisa on a regular." I rolled my eyes.

"Then, you come along and challenged him in Walmart right away which took us all by surprise. Somehow y'all continued running into one another and you had him stuck. You didn't back down and it made him want you more. My nephew was almost kidnapped and you stepping in, sealed the deal."

"Then why is he so mean? Why did he sleep with her? I thought we were doing fine." I felt my eyes becoming watery.

"It's no excuse as to why he did it. I can say, he must've realized it was wrong because he left her."

"Left her?"

"Yup. She ran out my house yelling about him leaving her in the middle of them having sex and why won't he be with her."

"He still shouldn't have done it." I rolled my eyes.

"I agree."

"Then the bitch comes to my job." Conscience waved me off and accepted her food.

"She's run off a few women by showing up at places they worked at and Consequence didn't care. The only difference now is, he doesn't wanna lose you. He doesn't want lil Con to lose you."

"I would never walk out on lil Con."

"You already did. Excuse me. I have to take this. Wrap my food up." She walked away to speak on the phone.

"What did you do Zakiya. I know you didn't leave his son hanging." I put my head down.

"I have to go ladies. It was nice chatting." She grabbed her things.

"Oh, and it's been a week since it happened and lil Con has called you almost every day. I know you're upset with my brother and I get it, but he's not ok with you going ghost on lil Con."

"I just needed a break from Consequence."

"He's not asking you to be his mother Zakiya, we all want you to be very clear on that." She said.

"I know and I never said you guys did."

"To lil Con, you saved him and because you're around a lot, he wants to keep you around."

"I'm going to call him."

"Listen, if you don't wanna be with my brother, that's fine. As you can see, lil Con misses you. If you can't honor that, then it's best you continue not answering and never come around again."

"Is the truck out front?" She asked her guard.

"I think you'd be a cool sister in law but know hurting my nephew or brothers, will have a bullet in between your eyes before you can ask why it happened."

"Did you just threaten me?" I snapped.

"I only make promises. Enjoy the rest of your day ladies." She hopped in a black SUV and disappeared.

"I don't know about you but I'm ready to go home." I said to Andrina.

"Courage is outside waiting for me." I nodded. We paid for our food and stepped outside the restaurant. Courage was directly in the front.

"I'll be by the house in a few to grab some things."

"Ok." I spoke to Courage and watched them pull off.

"Who the fuck?" I barked when someone put their hands over my eyes.

"ROCK!"

"The one and only baby."

CHAPTER 27

Consequence

"**D**addy can we go see Miss Zakiya?" My son asked.

"Yea but not right now. Nana wanted to see you." I handed him his phone and locked the door on our way out.

"I know but I miss Zakiya."

"How about this? I drop you off to nanas house and go pick Miss Zakiya up. I'm sure she's gonna be happy to see you."

"Fine. Can you at least have her face time me?" I hated what my son was going through. A lot of it is my fault because I hurt Zakiya, but she still came around when I was mean to her. Why isn't she speaking to my son? It's been long enough so I guess it's time to go see her. The least I can do, is apologize.

"Hey. Have you spoken to Courage or seen Rock?" My mom asked when we got there.

"No why?"

"Conscience called and said she's having pains and neither of them are answering."

"Courage probably with Drina. I'll go by and check." I let my son hand go and my mom grabbed my arm.

"Don't go over there cutting up."

"What you talking about?"

"If Zakiya is there, let her speak first. You hurt her bad Consequence." She folded her arms across her chest.

"I know."

"I hope you do because now it's affecting my grand baby." I blew my breath.

"I don't doubt she'll be by to see him. I just think she's taking some time to herself. However, if she is home, just ask her to contact me. I'll handle it from there."

"A'ight." I sat in my car thinking about what my mom said. I don't think Zakiya is intentionally tryna hurt lil Con. But women take much longer to move past things.

* * *

I parked outside Zakiya's house and instead of barging in like I normally would, I picked up my phone and called. It took her to the fourth ring to answer.

"I just spoke to lil Con."

"He's been tryna speak to you all week." She got quiet.

"I told you, you didn't have to be the mother figure in his life, but you did it anyway. Now my son is upset because you haven't answered his calls."

199

"I'm sorry. I was hurt by what you did and taking a break." I heard the pain in her voice.

"Ok but you could've picked him up from my parents."

"You're right and I apologize again. I just told your mom I'm going to pick him up tomorrow. I can't believe I messed up with him. I love your son." I appreciated the fact she admitted to messing up and that she spoke to him.

"Come outside." I heard noise in the background.

"Why are you outside my house?" I noticed the shades move in her living room window.

"Do I need to come in?"

"No." It took her a few minutes to open the door and when she did, I became angry. I hopped out my car and rushed to the door.

"Why you dressed like this?" I pulled at the shorts barely covering her ass and the tank top. Granted, she had a thick robe on but still. What if my brother in there?

"I'm home and you've seen me wear this before." She tightened the belt on the robe.

"Exactly and I took them right off and fucked you."

"Consequence please stop. You asked me to come out here and I did. What do you want?" She blocked me from going inside.

"I can't come in?"

"I have company."

"Why my girl got company?" She laughed.

"I believe your girl is Lisa and trust me, she's not here."

"I came by to apologize. I was dead ass wrong for

allowing her to touch me. You were my woman and I disrespected you, and us." Her head was down but I could hear her sniffling.

"I'm sorry Zakiya. I didn't mean to hurt you." I lifted her head and it was at this very moment, I knew I wanted; no, I needed her in my life. I wiped the tears from her eyes.

"Why Consequence? Was I not good enough? You could've told me." I hugged her tight.

"I just messed up Za. I let my dick think for me. It'll never happen again."

"You hurt me."

"I know and I promise to make it up to you." I hugged her again and let out a sigh when she hugged me back.

"Damn I missed you." I said lifting her face up for a kiss. I was surprised she allowed it to happen. Maybe the break she took made her realized, she needed me to. I swear if she takes me back, I'll never cheat again.

"Ummm. I have to tell you something." She kept her arms around my waist.

"What?"

"I didn't know he was here, and I wanted to tell you about him."

"Who? You didn't know who was here?" She moved away.

"Yo! I gotta go." Rock opened the door and my mind went crazy.

"Why is my sisters' man over here?"

"Your sister? Rock, you're with his sister?" Before he could respond, I placed the tip of my gun on Zakiya's forehead.

"What the fuck you doing Consequence?" Rock yelled. Zakiya put her hands up and backed herself into the house.

"Yo! Put that shit down." He yelled.

"I told you never to cheat on me."

"I didn't Consequence; I swear. Rock is..."

BOOM! I didn't even stay to watch her body drop.

To Be Continued...

Now Available on
Amazon

Made in United States
North Haven, CT
11 May 2024

52334770R00129